Freeing Fortune

A Novel

by
Ashley J. Barner
and
Jennifer Sanders

Cover design by Garrett Varady, Varady Visuals

Printed in the United States of America
First Printing, 2019

ISBN 978-1-7339834-2-6

Notus Publishing
10 Alleman Lane
Shippensburg, PA 17257

www.NotusBooks.com

For Carolyn Chapple Reed, who taught me to love Regency romance.

Chapter One

An Excerpt from Fortune's Folly by Belinda Burnworth, published 1813:

Clouds burst, skies flash, oh, dreadful hour!
More fiercely pours the storm!
Yet here one thought has still the power
To keep my bosom warm.
~ Lord Byron, 'Stanzas Composed During a Thunderstorm, 1809'

Araminta Cavanaugh startled fearfully, first at the sound of thunder and then at the untoward intrusion of Lord Byron—and his bosom—into her thoughts. Le diable boiteux *himself! How Aunt Virulea would rage if she knew! The rain beat heavily on the windows of the conservatory, streaking the glass and obscuring the view of the Herefordshire countryside; the wind howling across the fields provided a disapproving counterpoint* to the older woman's imperious scowl as she lectured her ward. Araminta bowed her head in submission.

"Wealth!" Aunt Virulea towered over her delicate niece, snapping her plum-colored bombazine skirt for emphasis. "It is your duty," she proclaimed regally, one stumpy finger aimed at Araminta's nose, "to save your family by an advantageous marriage. You are not wealthy, but you have other advantages," she added in a mercenary vein that offended Araminta's sensibilities. "You are the daughter of a gentleman. You are not unintelligent, and can be quite charming when you put your mind to it. But most of all," she concluded with emphasis, "you have beauty of face and figure. You must use these both—especially the latter—to your advantage. We shall have to see a French modiste." The naming of that immodest nationality was accompanied with a significant widening of Virulea's small, slightly protuberant eyes. Araminta's damask cheek deepened to scarlet at this evidence of coarseness. "Do not blush, child," Aunt Virulea rebuked her sharply. "The world has no place for softness, neither of heart nor head, and the sooner you make your mind up to it the happier we shall all be."

"But, Aunt, what of love?"

"Love? Pah!" Aunt Virulea declaimed scathingly. "The dream of a child, like fairies and bugbears. Speak not to me of love! No, my girl, you will use all your charms and allurements to ensnare a wealthy husband during the London Season, or I shall wash my hands of your entire family!" She swept regally from the room in a welter of aubergine fabric, leaving Araminta to cast herself upon the floor in an attitude of Utter Despair, weeping piteously (though not too loudly, as that tended to produce excess moisture about the nose, and she wasn't entirely certain where she'd left her handkerchief).

A loud rapping upon the outer door of the conservatory made her pause mid-sob and raise her head, her lovely eyes red with crying. "Hello, there!" a masculine voice called. "Shelter for the wanderer?"

Araminta rose and pulled open the door with alacrity—not even a field-hand should be left to freeze in weather like this!

But the figure who entered was no rustic.

—He was tall and broad of shoulder, though as his bottle-green coat was utterly soaked through it was easy enough to tell that he owed nothing to the artifice of Bond Street padding, and Araminta could feel her cheeks grow warm at this evidence of physical strength. His dark curls, onyx in the stormy afternoon light, dripped rivulets upon a face surely carved by an angelic sculptor: a broad, intelligent brow; high, aristocratic cheeks; dark, winged brows that Gabriel himself would envy; a mouth that spoke of both sense and sensitivity. And yet his eyes, which ought to have been the clear blue of Heaven, were black as the pit of Hades as his gaze swept over her feminine form.

He bowed, dripping on the parquet she had so recently vacated. "Fortune," he uttered in a voice as deeply thrilling as the rest of him. "Ben Fortune," he

7

repeated slowly, and with kindness. "And your name,
Miss...?"

"Araminta Cavanaugh," she faltered, her heart
pounding. She knew of him: 'Devil' Fortune, cynosure
of the Ton, newly returned from the Continent.

"Good to know the name of one's savioress, I
find," he said with a smile, both mischief and sunshine.
"It's coming down sideways out there. Does it often
blow up suddenly like this?"

Linnea Santiago sighed in sheer pleasure. Here
it was: the first meeting between Araminta Cavanaugh
and her enigmatic neighbor—to the legions of FF-Fans
across the globe, the beckoning portal into the Regency
world of authoress Belinda Burnworth and her most
noted hero, Ben Fortune. The *Pride and Prejudice* fans
could keep their Mr. Darcy: Linnea—and a host of other
readers—preferred Burnworth's tantalizing 'Devil'
Fortune, with his dark good looks and mysterious ways.
There was somehow more to him than the standard
Heathcliff-style Regency hero: witness the description
of that smile, for example. Ben Fortune was not easily
categorized—or forgotten.

Linnea eagerly turned the page, remembering at
the last to actually chew and swallow the bite of
sandwich in her mouth. So engrossed was she in the
novel that she jumped when she realized someone was
speaking to her.

"Mind if I join you?" The speaker was a young woman, about Linnea's own age, juggling a plate of salad. "All the other tables seem to be full."

Returned to reality for a moment, Linnea looked around. It was true—her favorite coffee shop, Bookish Brews, seemed to be filled to capacity with other grad students vying for a moment's respite from the grind of academic research. "Oh—yeah, of course! Sorry," Linnea added, moving her purse to the floor to make room for the other woman. "I was engrossed in my book." She flashed the cover at her.

"Oh, *Fortune's Folly!*" The woman's eyes lit up as she took the seat. "That's my *favorite!*"

Linnea laughed, trying not to get mayo on the cover of her dog-eared paperback. "Then you're *doubly* welcome. Linnea Santiago," she held out her hand, somewhat awkwardly.

Her new companion took it. "Susan Hu. You're a... grad student?" she guessed.

Linnea chuckled. Not much of a leap, since 'Bookie B's' was actually located on Sunhill University's campus. "Mmhm. History. You?"

"English," Susan grinned, starting in on her salad. "I'm actually thinking about doing my dissertation partly on *Fortune's Folly*. My adviser is a *massive* Araminta fangirl. I might do a chapter on it."

That surprised a full-bodied laugh out of Linnea. "Oh, if only—I'd have the whole thing memorized already. What's your favorite bit? No—fifth favorite, then we can work our way up."

Susan laughed, too. "I don't think I could rank them without a spreadsheet. I *do* love the scene where Fortune and Araminta meet for the first time. Wet t-shirt contest! Woohoo!"

"I was *just* reading that scene!" Linnea gurgled with laughter. "Burnworth did seem to love wet shirt scenes, since she wrote *two* of them in the same book! ...Okay, we have to establish something here: are you pro-movie or anti-movie?"

"I *think* I like Tom Hattleson as Fortune," Susan said slowly, "but I'm kind of worried about how they might write him, that they might make him more of an asshole than he really was. Like Faramir in *Lord of the Rings*."

"*Yes!*" Linnea slammed her hand on the table. "Also, not to be cruel to Hattleson—he seems a lovely guy—but I just don't see him as Ben Fortune, personally. He's not... *macho* enough. Fortune should be so much man it can't even be contained, you know?" She took a bite of her sandwich, hiding her mouth with her hand as she went on. "Though I liked the scene in the trailer where he tells Araminta how he feels about her: 'My dear girl, my feelings for you—you must have been mistook' and all the while his face is saying, 'Look, if there was a bed in the room...'"

Susan nodded eagerly. "Yes! Like that *Pride and Prejudice* movie scene in the rain, where Darcy and Elizabeth are all mad and then they almost kiss... Yeah. It looks like it could be really good. Hope so, anyway."

She ate a forkful of salad. "So you said history: do you study the Regency era?"

"Long eighteenth century, which includes the Regency, though my concentration is on John Key."

"John Key..." Susan narrowed her eyes in thought, clearly recognizing the name. "Is he a... philosopher?"

Linnea nodded, amused. "If you asked him he'd say yes, along with about a hundred other bloody things. He's a polymath, an essayist, one of those guys who sits in the corner ruminating, hollers 'aha!', writes a monograph, and is hailed by royalty. Except the one on the digestive properties of various colors of food. That one got a solid boo from the populace."

"So what are you interested in from his writings?"

"Well," Linnea took a deep breath, "Sunhill is in possession of the largest extant collection of Keysiana. It's got a lot of material in it. And let me tell you, that's like saying the polar ice cap has a lot of snow." She shook her head. "So I've been working for Dr. Helman, who's a Keysian scholar, trying to get it catalogued. Or some portion of it catalogued. I'm hoping Dr. H will wind up as my dissertation adviser, but like Winnie the Pooh once said, one never can tell with bees."

"Wow, archival work has always sounded so interesting to me. And at least you've got plenty of material to work from!"

"You don't know the half of it," Linnea returned darkly. "Personally, I think Janky's heirs must have taken one look at everything and decided the solution was either donation or arson. Donation was just the more legal of the two. And at least this way they get bragging rights for having an ancestor with a university collection in his name."

Susan chuckled. "'Janky'? Is that shorthand for John Key?" Linnea nodded, sipping her drink. "So what attracted you to studying this guy, if he's such a crackpot?"

"Just that—the crackpot angle. The thing is," Linnea leaned forward, "he's a *fascinating* crackpot. There's everything in there—it's a treasure trove of folklore and folk beliefs from all over England, and I'm hoping to find something interesting to write about for my diss. Something like the Green Children of Woolpit, for instance, or the Pied Piper of Hameln. There's one tale that John Key was at a dinner party where he pulled a fictional character out of a novel and introduced him to the other guests!" Susan began to giggle. Linnea grinned in response. "I know, right? But apparently the character got upset, and Key sent him back to fiction-land. The scholarship will tell you it's all a metaphor, but the conspiracy theorists aren't so sure." She shook her head. "It's amazing stuff, once you get through all the cricket scores and meteorological statistics and laundry lists. The man kept *everything*. And that's leaving out the marginalia."

"Like what?" Susan asked, still clearly amused.

"Bizarre little notes, scribbles, sketches... It's sometimes more interesting than the essays themselves!

Tantalizing," Linnea concluded, and picked up her sandwich. "Enough Janky. So tell me about your diss."

"Oh—well," Susan began, "it's on shadow narratives. Like how in Austen's *Emma*, Jane Fairfax has a story that's almost more interesting than Emma's? I'm writing about those."

"Oh, now that's a *cool* premise. I always wondered why Jane Fairfax was never a point-of-view character—I would've loved to get into her tidy little head just once. So who else?"

"Well, there are a couple of options in *Fortune's Folly*. I mean, obviously the suspense in the story is based on the fact that Araminta doesn't know why Ben Fortune won't marry her even though he's clearly in love with her. But wouldn't it be interesting to see that conflict from *his* point of view instead of hers? It's a little like Elinor Dashwood in *Sense and Sensibility,* spending most of the plot just *reacting* because it's the man she's in love with who has all the interesting adventures."

"Yes, and all offscreen, as it were." Linnea rested her chin in her hands. "So why do you think he never asked Araminta to marry him? Do you believe in the fable of the mysterious bride?"

Susan shook her head. "I think Burnworth wanted to show him as a mixture of too shy and too proud to declare his love—like Darcy, only even more resisting. A casualty of his own nature, as it were. Nonetheless," she added, grinning mischievously, "I kind of like the theory that he lost his family's fortune by gambling and has to marry a rich bride."

"Except we never see him court anyone else. Personally I like to think he's saving himself for me." Linnea wiggled her eyebrows and ate her pickle.

"I would fight you for him, but I think my girlfriend would have something to say about that," Susan chuckled.

Linnea joined in her laughter, and then her phone alarm went off. "Nuts, I have to get back to the oubliette. I'm so glad you sat here—it's always great to meet a fellow FF-Fan. Would you and your girlfriend like to meet for coffee sometime, maybe?"

"Yeah, that'd be great!" Susan smiled. "Linnea... Santiago, was it? I'll look you up on Faceplace."

"Awesome—talk soon, I hope." Linnea waved a goodbye as she picked up her things and headed back to the archive.

Chapter Two

Linnea Santiago opened the door to the rooms dedicated to the John Key collection and immediately found herself knee-deep once more in a tsunami of papers that her adviser called "the workings of the greatest philosophical mind of the eighteenth century" and an irritated fellow scholar had once characterized as "absolute twaddle-poop of the most turgid kind": John Key's papers.

The larger of the two rooms was crammed to the ceiling with boxes, chests, old suitcases, plastic bins, crumbling leather folders tied with musty old string... And Linnea's favorite, a portrait of the man himself. It wasn't original—the trustees would have had a collective heart attack, comprised of either joy or terror at the responsibility. But there it was, perched atop one of the boxes as if to greet her each time she came into the room, his watery-blue eyes slightly protuberant under his velvet doctoral cap, fuzzy brows high, his lower lip slack as though to ask how on earth she'd gotten into the room? Sometimes, looking at the paths she had had to clear in the mess, she wondered that herself: the place was beginning to look like a hedge maze.

Dr. Helman had sweet-talked John Key's descendants into donating the collection twenty years ago—though the mind rather boggled at the image of Jack Helman sweet-talking anyone into anything. It was more likely that he talked their ear off until they acquiesced out of sheer self-preservation.

Since then, a long lineage of Helman's research assistants—desperate, hardy, deluded souls, one after another—had been slogging their way through, cataloguing everything except the occasional desiccated mouse skeleton. The pit of despair, Linnea's predecessor Billy Shanks had called it, and that was only one of the epithets the research room had been landed with over the years.

"The man kept *everything*," Billy had told her when he was showing her the ropes right after she had taken over his position. "A list of the number of crows he saw in a week, some highly suspect 'Laws and Customs of the Formosans'… You be careful," he added, pointing at her with a monitory finger. "You know how they say med students start to think they've got every disease they study?" He made a noise rather like 'tcha!', then went on. "Well, *your* biggest threat is Jankyism. Anybody who studies his ephemera starts to think there are deep, dark, symbolic secrets hidden in every word he writes. Look at this," he added, pulling out a notebook and flipping it open. "Little geometrical drawings, lists of names, a couple of random numbers, and a scribble that might be a face. I guarantee you, it means absolutely nothing. But stare at it too long, and you'll start to think it's showing you a map to the Fountain of Youth or something. Dr. Helman suffers from the worst case of Jankyism I've ever seen." He tossed the eighteenth-century notebook aside with a carelessness that made Linnea wince.

Linnea had been tempted to tell the practical-minded Billy Shanks that it was John Key's occult esoterica that had first attracted her to Keysian studies. She didn't hold with the conspiracy theorists, but she loved that Keys, an eighteenth-century Renaissance man, had been interested in everything from geological surveys to the possible origins of Stonehenge. And the crazier the writing got, the better Linnea liked it—though it probably wouldn't make very good dissertation material, unfortunately.

And then there was the problem of Dr. Helman himself. He was obviously the first choice as a dissertation adviser, and Billy Shanks had proven to be right on one thing: the good scholar was dancing along the perimeter of the Land of Conspiracy, where lay Elvis sightings and anti-vaxxers. If Linnea *did* find a subject in the archives that was weird enough for her to enjoy writing her dissertation, Dr. Helman would probably take one look at it and dive straight off the grassy knoll into *Da Vinci Code* territory.

Linnea settled back down to work, grabbing box 24D and glancing through its contents. One of the most interesting was a leather-bound commonplace book, so

Linnea grabbed a pencil and numbered the pages, then startled cataloging the contents, page by page. She had long ago learned to read John Key's rather idiosyncratic handwriting, and had even decoded a number of his usual abbreviations, so the cataloging went much faster than it had the first couple of months in the archives.

There was an unusual little essay, copied out in the good copperplate writing he used when he had a full draft. It dealt with realism in fictional characters, with a great deal of reference to Samuel Richardson's *Pamela* and *Clarissa*.

Unusually for one of his full-draft essays, this one had a great deal of marginalia. Linnea, who always had an eye out for anything unusual that she might be able to analyze, snapped pictures of the pages with her cell phone. She had dozens of these archive photos on her phone: some of them were research, but she also took pictures of anything funny she ran across—like Janky's little tirade on the more inelegant root vegetables. Whenever Linnea was feeling down, all she had to do was pull up "A Few Observations on That Most Inedible and Unappealing Crop, the Mangle-Wurzel" to get a good laugh.

At long last it was five-thirty, and Linnea tidied up her workspace and stuck a bookmark in the commonplace book. She locked the archive door and checked her phone as she headed toward her car, smiling when she saw that Susan Hu had already friended her—and sent her a Burnworth meme.

Back at the apartment, Linnea read some more of *Fortune's Folly*, skipping forward to read her favorite scenes as she reheated some pizza for dinner. This time, as she read, Linnea couldn't help but wonder what Ben Fortune was thinking—how the story would be changed if it had been narrated from his point of view instead of Araminta's.

Araminta and her aunt greeted their hostess, Lady Goodcompany, and joined the crush in the overheated ballroom. Despite the fullness of the room, both men and women drew back at their approach, and Araminta could not help but blush at the gazes of warm regard from the gentlemen—and the jealous glances of the ladies as they took in Araminta's pink toilette with spider gauze and garnet parure, a glimmering garnet aigrette in her guinea-gold curls. One young lady had attempted to wear a similar shade, but it made her look sadly sallow, and she would not meet Araminta's gaze.

Araminta also avoided acknowledging Mr. Fortune's Uncle, Mr. Moribund Fortune, and his crony, Captain Wambold: it would do her no good to be seen conversing with two men of such terrible reputation. How such a man as Mr. Fortune could be so unlucky as to have such undesirable connexions... But she had never heard anything specific to condemn Mr. Fortune himself, apart from that unfortunate nickname. Quite the reverse: though reserved, he was never other than gentlemanly.

Araminta's blushes continued when Aunt Virulea plucked a wealthy, diffident young man from the crowd to partner her niece in the country dance, most certainly interrupting old Colonel Braveit, whose eyes when they rested on Araminta seemed to be reviewing his younger days with such joy. Young Lord Dashington disclaimed any ability to partner her as she deserved, but as Araminta knew he was an excellent dancer, she merely smiled kindly upon him, hoping he would forgive her aunt's vulgarity.

As young Lord Dashington escorted her onto the floor, Araminta's gaze caught a pair of dark, devilish eyes in an astoundingly handsome masculine face: Mr. Fortune was there.

But as Araminta moved her head to watch him, he looked away, turning quickly to speak to the young man beside him. He was intentionally avoiding her. But why? His words, his gaze, when last they had seen one another had been unmistakable. He had surely been on the verge of making a declaration—if only his cousin the Viscount had not interrupted him.

Araminta paid only the minutest attention to the dance and answered her poor partner at random. Surely, she felt, Mr. Fortune would seek her out for the quadrille? But Mr. Fortune remained resolutely on the other side of the room, as if knowing that any closer proximity to her would endanger his resolve.

Indeed, he seemed unable to meet her eye, looking away every time it happened upon accident. At every nearly-shared glance she felt an electric jolt: even from across the room, the strength of his feelings was obvious.

The sound of her roommate's bedroom door opening caught her attention. "That had best not be the microwave I hear," Kurt's familiar baritone floated down the hall.

"Whyever not?" Linnea called back as he came into the kitchen.

"Because I wanted Chinese takeout." Kurtis Walton ran his hands over his close-cropped dark head as he plopped into a seat at the kitchen table, his long legs taking up half the floor.

"You can still get Chinese takeout," Linnea said, pulling the pizza from the microwave and pouring herself some lemonade.

"Since when is Chinese takeout any fun for one person? Plus, they always send you two fortune cookies and then I'm left with the extra one. And you can't have two fortunes; it's illegal. And against the laws of nature."

Linnea laughed. "Of course."

"You think I'm kidding?" Kurt opened his eyes very wide as he stole her plate of pizza and stuck it back in the fridge. "One time my cousin Deshawn ate two fortune cookies, and the next day, he made an omelet that had two yolks in it."

"That sounds delicious. And you're wasting my pizza! It's going to taste weird if I reheat it again."

"Pizza always tastes weird if you reheat it in the microwave anyway, and yeah, it was a pretty good omelet." Kurt slipped his arm around her waist and dipped her backward. "Please, Linnea, I'm begging you—save me from the curse of the lonely man's Moo Goo Gai Pan. Last time I had Chinese by myself I couldn't get a date for a week. Is that the kind of fate you're willing to condemn me to?"

She was laughing again. "I already spent my eating-out money this week on the pizza!"

Kurt grinned. "Was I unclear? The Moo Goo Gai Pan will be on me. Figuratively, of course, unless you think you can handle," he gestured to himself with the arm she wasn't dangling from, "all this."

"Never!" She pressed the back of one hand to her forehead. "You are too much man for me, Kurt Walton!"

"Truer words, woman. But you're still not going to make me Moo Goo by myself, are you? I'll spring for wine..."

"Well, if you *insist* on plying me with Chinese takeout and wine, who am I to cavil?" Linnea batted her eyelashes innocently. "I only hope you're not planning on taking advantage of me once I'm full of Sweet and Sour Chicken."

He dropped her onto the sofa without ceremony and went to rummage through the takeout menus. "Who, me?"

"Yes, you, Sir Chivalry." She struggled to get up from the deep sofa cushions. "Last time you took advantage of my innocence by challenging me to a game of Monopoly."

He had his phone to his face. "Mm. Reminds me, you still owe me back rent on Park Place. Sweet and sour, you said?"

"Make it General Tso's. It was just too dirty to say in context."

That cracked him up. He placed the order and then spread himself all over the sofa like peanut butter. "So how was your day, dear?"

She shrugged. "The usual. Oh, I met a fellow *Fortune's Folly* fan at lunch!"

He rolled his eyes. "Oh, Bucephalus," he warbled, "you steamy, sexy hunk of man without enough sense to carry an umbrella in the rain. Come make love to me on the conservatory floor while Aunt Influenza searches for her lorgnette, which I have cleverly misplaced in a ruse to get you alone."

Linnea cackled loudly. "Aunt Influenza??"

"Something stupid like that, anyway. Aunt Varicella."

"Virulea!" Linnea was still chortling.

"Of course. And who names their hero Mr. Follicle?"

"FORTUNE. You know, *'Fortune's Folly'*?"

Kurt grinned and nudged her foot with his own. "I know—it's all about his luxurious hair: Fortune's Follicles. Oh, shoot. I need to get some laundry done." He ran off to gather up his clothes and stuff them in the washer. In a short time the bell rang, signifying the arrival of their food, and Kurt stopped needling Linnea long enough to stuff his face, then returned immediately to the fray, snatching up her book and flipping through it.

"*Oh, Mr. Fortune!*" he read. "*I'm afraid I may have sprained my ankle!*"

"Give me that." Linnea made a snatch for the book, but Kurt held it out of her reach.

"*Fortune paused a moment, then made his way toward her, his countenance full of concern. 'Are you able to walk upon it, Miss Cavanaugh?'*" He was doing voices for the characters: a faint falsetto for Araminta and a sweepingly dramatic bass for Fortune. Linnea started laughing.

"I would act out the bit where he carries her back to her house, but I'm busy eating," Kurt said conscientiously, and flipped onward. "Ah, here we are. *Fortune set Araminta gently down upon the paving stones. He pounded upon the door. "Ho! The house! Help for Miss Cavanaugh!"*

Araminta wrapped her thin shawl more tightly about herself, her white walking gown dripping with the rain. Her ankle felt swollen already.

There was a sound of footsteps inside, and then John, the footman, opened the door. "Oh, Miss!" he cried in great concern.

Fortune swept her up in his arms once more. "Where is her bedroom?" he asked the footman, who hurried ahead of him to show him the way. Araminta blushed and trembled as he carried her into her boudoir and set her gently upon her bed."

"Okay, enough dramatic reading." With an air of triumph Linnea finally succeeded in getting her book back from him. "If I keep laughing like this while I'm eating, I'm going to be sick."

"Nah, come on, Araminta," Kurt urged. "See if you can keep up with me." He pointed to the next line on the page.

She giggled, but joined in gamely. "*He sat beside her upon the counterpane,*" she read dramatically. "'*Forgive me—I must just see whether the bone is sound or if the doctor should be called for.' Araminta suppressed a squeak as his large palms came in contact with her stocking, and nearly fainted at the liberty he took, his fingertips lightly caressing the arch of her foot.*"

Kurt took up the thread, tickling Linnea's foot, laughing when she smacked his hand away. "*The door exploded inward to reveal Aunt Virulea, so in a fury that her hair was like to come off through sheer combustion. 'And what is this?' she declaimed in her best Mrs. Siddons style. 'A rogue,' complete with rolling 'r', 'come to debauch my gentle Araminta under my own roof—nay, in her own bed? They do not call you Devil Fortune for naught, I see.'*" He gave Aunt Virulea a comic British accent, his voice honking like a lovelorn goose with every other word.

Fortune's eyes grew dark indeed; Araminta found herself unable to decipher the roiling emotions she read upon his sinfully handsome face. "I assure you, madam, that your daughter-"

"Niece," Virulea flatly corrected him.

"Niece, yes, whichever—the poor young lady chanced to fall and turn her ankle. Observing her mishap, I picked her up and brought her here as soon as I might."

"You brought her, in your own arms, to her boudoir to complete her debauchery. Had she merely turned her ankle you could have sent for a carriage." Aunt Virulea snapped open her lorgnette and looked the dripping-wet gentleman up and down.

"Madam, I am sure it has not escaped your notice that the downpour outside your window seems to have challenged the deluge for sheer volume. My only thought was to get her home, and safely, without more loss of time. And having done so," Fortune tipped his hat, from which an impressive rivulet poured upon the carpet, "I take my leave of you both."

"Halt!" cried Aunt Virulea. "What assurance have I that my Araminta is as intact a maiden now as she was when she met you?"

Araminta was ready to sink. What could her aunt be thinking, making such accusations?

Dark, winged brows took nearly to the sky. "There is the circumstance of this footman, who did not leave us alone for a moment," he began mildly, "and the further circumstance that I still wear my greatcoat, and it is soaked through. Generally, when bent upon seduction, saturated outerwear is considered a *hindrance, especially when speed seems to be of the essence. Most importantly, there is the word of the lady herself." He nodded at Araminta, who turned crimson.*

"He only touched my ankle, Aunt, to see whether it was broken," Araminta hurried to affirm. "And my calf, and the arch of my foot..." she added somewhat dreamily.

Out came Mrs. Siddons again. "You removed an article of my niece's clothing?"

"Well—I mean to say—her shoe," Fortune faltered.

The lorgnette examined him minutely, focusing on the cut of his sodden coat, the gold fob-chain at his waist; and suddenly Aunt Virulea's intent did an about-face that Boney's soldiers could not have bettered. She smiled terrifyingly. "La, sir! Of course you need stand on no ceremony with us, as we are neighbors. You will forgive my tone just now," and it was more an order than a request, "but naturally you understand that one cannot be too careful in these days of sin and vice. I assure you I take my responsibility to Araminta quite seriously."

"I believe you," he said, a droll quirk to his lips.

"But of course I know she need fear nothing from you, *excepting all of the attention such a flower is due from a gentleman. You," again she emphasized the pronoun quite uncomfortably, "I am sure, could never take such advantage of my Araminta, pressing her innocence without the proper intentions."*

He blanched visibly, and Araminta wanted to protest. Was Aunt attempting to secure an offer of marriage on the spot? How reluctant Mr. Fortune would be to reveal the true depths of his feelings for her after such dreadful accusations!

Indeed, "I would not," he agreed instead of declaring undying love. "Let me further assure you, Miss Cavanaugh—"

"Bah!" Araminta's aunt waved a decisive hand. "I have declared you owe me no such assurances, and I will accept none! Let us only say we understand one another completely, hm?"

"Miss Cavanaugh, I must insist—"

"Sir, it is I who insist, and I believe I have the right of both age and sex to overrule you in this case!" She simpered. "And now I believe I must just see Araminta into dry clothing. A good afternoon, sir."

Thus dismissed, Mr. Fortune bowed to Aunt Virulea, and then to Araminta before he left, his dark gaze unreadable. A thrill ran down Araminta's spine. Did he mean to—had he been going to—would she have allowed it if he had...?

"Araminta!" thundered her aunt.

"Yes, Aunt Virulea?"

"You will cease thinking at once!"

Araminta sighed. "Yes, Aunt Virulea."

Kurt couldn't stand it any longer and went off in peals of laughter. "Alright, I think I'm starting to see the appeal of this book," he said, handing it back to Linnea.

"This Araminta character's a trip and a half. My favorite's Aunt Virulea, though."

"Araminta's not that bad," Linnea grinned as her friend dug into his Moo Goo Gai Pan again.

"So who's this chick you met?" Kurt asked with his mouth full. "She cute?"

"Her name is Susan Hu, she's cute, and she's taken." Linnea returned her attention to her General Tso's chicken. "How was *your* day? Or night, I should say." Kurt was working a night shift on his residency at the local hospital.

He lifted a shoulder. "The usual. A kid who put his arm through a sliding glass door, a frat boy who heard an urban legend about a toothbrush and wanted to prove it wasn't true, some idiot who decided to make homemade fireworks, couple other things. You?"

"I'm not even going to ask about the toothbrush."

"Yeah, you really don't want to know. It was the vibrating kind."

"Oh, God." She buried her face in her hand. "Aaaaand now I know."

Her roommate chuckled. "You working tonight, or want to watch a movie?"

"Ugggggh. I want to watch a movie, but I really should get something done. Specifically, I need to go back through some of my notes from the archive and see if I can get any dissertation ideas."

"I thought you couldn't bring anything out of there."

She waved her phone. "I can't. But they never specifically told me I couldn't bring home photos!"

"Oh yeah?" He leaned over her shoulder. "You keep saying how bad this guy Janky's writing is—lemme see."

She pulled up a photo. "Here's one I took today."

Kurt squinted. "And that's English, is it?"

"Yep." She zoomed in. "Look, here it says, '*Thus through the mechanism of sympathy do we bring alive in our bodies the sensations of the hero.*'"

He tilted his head this way and that. "If you say so. What's the doodle for?"

"*That*," she said impressively, "is a *manicule*."

"Manicule... like manicure? Because its little nails are done?"

She chuckled. "Well, yeah, they're really pointy, but it's called a manicule because it's a little 'manus'—a hand. People used to draw them in the margins to indicate important passages. Like an old-fashioned highlighter pen."

Kurt studied it a moment longer. "So he wanted to emphasize that word, or line or whatever."

"Yeah, I guess." She frowned at it. "I don't know why, though. And it's weird for him to have put manicules on this essay. Not like him."

"What word is it?"

"Um... book." She shook her head. "Well, the whole essay's about books; why would he point to that word?"

Kurt chewed on his lip. "Why's the word capitalized? It's not the beginning of the sentence. Do they do that a lot with nouns?"

"Yes, actually. Like German. Then eventually they just capitalized Important Words."

He scanned the document. "Oh I see. Like that one. It has a manicule too." Kurt scratched his lip. "Seems like a lot of extra work, though, capitalizing and then drawing hands to make sure you didn't miss the capital letter, I guess." He shook his head. "Better you than me, Linnea. I don't even like Scrabble."

"Me neither," she said absently, tapping her finger on the table. "But I think I'm going to take a look at this—see if I can figure out what he's getting at."

"You have fun with that," her roommate said teasingly. "I'm going to surf the 'net for a while, see what everyone's up to. Maybe play some Terminal Head Trip XV." Kurt plopped down on the couch and dragged out his laptop.

Linnea pulled out a notebook and a pen and began examining the photos. First she looked to see if it was the passage or the line the manicule seemed to be pointing to, and tried to make sense of that: but there was no sense to be made.

But Kurt was right; the hands always pointed to capitalized words—so maybe it was the words Key was indicating? It was beginning to get into Conspiracy Land, but worth a try. Linnea jotted down the words the hands were pointing to... and lo and behold, they came out in complete sentences.

She barely came out of her Janky-induced stupor when Kurt interrupted the silence. "Hey, Linnea!"

"Yeah?"

"I'm gonna make a video game shooter out of your boyfriend!"

"My boyfriend?" She glanced up, confused.

"Yeah, the conservatory seduction artist!" This was followed by a long cackle.

It took her a second to catch on. "You do that," she answered, rolling her eyes. This code, if code it was, was pretty fascinating, and beautifully worded. She read it off in a murmur, savoring the sound of it. "... *For true you are, though made of words. And so I call thee forth from the pages—*"

"What's his full name again?" asked Kurt.

"Ben Fortune!" she answered automatically. Then there was that final, mysterious Latin word: "*Praevaleo.*"

There was a cracking noise, and Linnea's inner ears pulsed, like the air pressure in the room had suddenly changed. She looked up—and froze.

Pounding upon their front door, as though looking to escape, was a man Linnea had never seen before—or had she?

He was soaked to the skin and shivering. "Ho! The house! Help for Miss Cavanaugh!" he cried in a husky baritone, then went still as he took in his surroundings.

Linnea stared just as hard as the newcomer did. His high-collared white shirt was plastered to him, the cutaway coat he wore glistening black and dripping onto his vest. His ebony hair was stuck to his face in ducktails, and his face...

His face. *"...Surely carved by an angelic sculptor: a broad, intelligent brow; high, aristocratic cheeks; dark, winged brows that Gabriel himself would envy; a mouth that spoke of both sense and sensitivity. And yet his eyes, which ought to have been the clear blue of Heaven, were black as the pit of Hades."*

"Ben Fortune," Linnea breathed.

Chapter Three

Ben Fortune stood stock still, trying to take in his surroundings, eyes darting about. Where was the greenhouse—the path—Miss Cavanaugh? He blinked. Had his eyesight suddenly given way? Or his mind? He was—indoors, but in a room totally unfamiliar to him, with its flat, painted walls, strange furnishings, and... even stranger people.

One of them, a dark-skinned man near Ben's own age, hair shaved close, dark brows and mouth drawn in a deep frown, came toward him, his mien... uncongenial. Ben tried not to flinch. "How the hell did you get in here?" the strange man demanded, moving in front of the woman protectively. "And why the hell are you wet?"

Why was he...? "But—it is raining quite hard out!" he answered automatically. Behind the man, the young woman stepped forward, her dark eyes wide and unblinking, like a doe in sudden sunlight. She moved as though in a trance, her gaze locked firmly on Ben, and... had she said his *name*?

She reached out and tugged on the other man's arm. "It's him," she hissed.

"Him who?" her companion muttered back, just as though Ben himself were not standing in front of them. The girl whispered in her companion's ear and he blinked. "Come off it, Hermione. How's a character from a novel going to show up in our living room like—like one of those Las Vegas acts, only without the tiger?" He glanced at Ben. "It's not raining," he pointed out.

"Not—" Ben was utterly bewildered, unable to understand. Tigers? Acts? "But I assure you, it was pouring a moment ago, and—" He cracked open the door beside him to find an utterly unfamiliar landscape, the air warm and relatively dry. Ben jammed his fingers into his sodden hair. He had slipped, perhaps: hit his head, scrambled his brains. But he felt uninjured, though that was perhaps a very symptom of his condition. "And I am clearly going mad. What is happening to me?"

Ben glanced back at the pair watching him. The man had relaxed significantly from his initial stance, and was returning Ben's scrutiny with undisguised curiosity. The young woman, despite the shocking view of her nether limbs clad in trousers, possessed a lovely face, though it would not have passed muster in many a boring social salon, given the unfashionable golden brown of her skin. Yet her features were finely drawn, her eyes—to which he could not help returning—were a warm, rich cognac, with the same golden gleam as her skin. Her mouth was perhaps a shade too full for

35

acceptability, which to Ben's eye made it all the more appealing. Her dark brown hair hung in glossy waves.

He became aware that he was staring in a most ungentlemanlike manner, and dropped his gaze.

"You're... um..." The woman—Hermione, had her companion called her? —seemed to stammer a bit. "Well... so I found this magic spell..."

Ben felt his brows climb. Was she claiming...? He cleared his throat. "I beg pardon—I thought I heard you say 'magic spell'?"

"Yeah. ...I did. I said magic spell. And it—it brought you here. I'm sorry."

Ben Fortune regarded himself as the most rational of men, and yet... Perhaps it *was* all a dream, but he could *feel* the chills of water trickling down his spine, dripping down the sides of his face. A rational man would know that in a dream one did not *feel*—not truly. But just to be sure, Ben surreptitiously pinched his thigh.

This was *not* a dream.

"I—you—" All of a sudden, he sneezed, shivering, and the other man changed demeanor entirely, his intelligent gaze reflecting concern.

"Come on, let's get you some dry clothes and get you warmed up, okay? And then we can figure this stuff out." Ben was conscious of being examined with a practiced eye. "Your lips are a bit blue, so a hot shower first. Linnea, get him a set of clean towels—I got the rest of this." With that Ben found himself being efficiently herded into another room, the door closing behind them.

Instead of getting the towels, Linnea dropped onto the couch, stunned. It took a few moments for her brain to formulate any thoughts at all. She'd done magic. With one of Janky's notebooks. He *did* have magical stuff in there! She began to laugh hysterically, and then stuffed a sofa pillow over her mouth to muffle the sound.

It was too bad she couldn't tell Dr. Helman. She couldn't tell *anybody*. They would think she was nuts. And even if she convinced them, what kind of chaos might ensue from the ability to pull fictional characters out of books?

And how did it happen, anyway? The answer came after a few moments: it must have been that she said Ben Fortune's name in the middle of the spell. Oh, Lord, this was a *mess*.

He *was* hot, though, her mind added inappropriately. Exactly as she'd imagined him. Talk about too much man: that broad chest, those black curls and even blacker eyes… Suddenly she started giggling. What would Susan—or any other diehard *Fortune's Folly* fan—think of this?

"Towels!" came the demand from the direction of the bathroom. "Come on, Lin!"

Oops! Linnea sprang up and went to fetch them, knocking at the door of the bathroom with two of them and a couple of washcloths. He was from the Regency— he might be *very* dirty, rain bath or no. She huffed out a wry breath.

She caught muffled snatches of Kurt's instructions on how to use the shower, the bath gel, and the toilet, and decided to get out of Dodge just as Kurt slipped out of the bathroom door, closing it carefully behind him. Linnea handed him the towels. "So, uh..."

"Couldn't have said it better myself. Linnea, what'd we *do*?"

"Well, it was mostly me," she said shamefacedly. "I found a code—the manicules *were* pointing out special words, and when I read them off, I guess it made a... a spell? And I said Ben Fortune's name in the middle of it, and... well... here he is?" She chewed her thumbnail guiltily.

Kurt snorted. "Putting aside the very improbable nature of everything you just said, it's not going to help much if you spend a lot of time beating yourself over the head with this. It's not like it would have occurred to anyone but a couple of nut jobs that this was going to actually *work*. Not that it wouldn't have been convenient to know beforehand, but: not the point."

"Okay, okay. Well—what do we do with him?" Linnea asked worriedly as she followed Kurt to his room.

"Figure out how to put him back, is my initial response, although maybe it's like the prime directive in *Star Trek* and he knows too much about the future." Kurt began pulling clothes from his dresser.

"He's from a fictional work," Linnea pointed out. "It's not like it's going to cause a paradox. I guess I

38

could go to the archive and look for more information in Janky's notebook..." she added doubtfully.

"Yeah, just... don't read anything else out loud."

The bathroom door opened enough for Fortune's dripping head to peek out. "If you please," he ventured, "what ought I to do now?"

Linnea gave a little gasp and turned her back quickly in case the rest of him came out as well. Kurt snorted again and gave him the towels and the clothes. "Here—you can wear these. Ought to be comfortable enough to sleep in. And this is deodorant—" was the last thing she heard as the door closed again. Linnea blew her cheeks out and went back to the living room to wait.

Eventually Kurt returned to the living room with a very different Ben Fortune in tow. Kurt was a tall, thin guy; Fortune was also surprisingly tall for his time period, and almost comically broad for Kurt's castoff t-shirt, which pulled across his chest and shoulders, his biceps straining the thin material. His dark hair was wet, tumbling across his brow and taking half of Linnea's attention with it. She stared, speechless, for a long moment. Kurt leaned over, stuck one finger under her chin, and pushed her mouth closed.

"I believe you have the advantage of me," Fortune said, somewhat uncertainly. "I heard you speak my name upon my rather unorthodox arrival, and yet I still do not know yours."

"Oh. Sorry. I'm Linnea Santiago," she answered, standing up and putting out her hand.

He glanced at it, then up at Kurt before taking her hand and pressing his lips gently to her knuckles. "Too antiquated?" he asked the other man.

Kurt chuckled. "Generally speaking, yeah, but I don't think she minded."

Linnea's cheeks were burning, and she had to force herself not to gape again as she retrieved her hand. "So you—" She cleared her throat and turned to Kurt. "You explained?"

Her roommate shrugged. "Sorta. Not like we understand that much anyway—just that somehow we've brought him to the future. And the US."

So he hadn't explained the fiction part yet. That was probably good. "We're going to look for a way to send you back," she promised.

"Not too soon, I hope," was his reply, accompanied by a smile that not even Belinda Burnworth's prose could do justice to.

"Oh, you—you like the future?" Linnea realized they were all still standing, and took a chair, gesturing to another one so he would feel free to sit. This had to be the weirdest small talk ever.

He laughed, teeth white in his handsome face. "Well, I've hardly sampled much of it, to this point; but the shower was a revelation. I should hate to leave before experiencing more." He tested Kurt's running shoe, slipping it on his foot. "What are these *made* of?"

"Plastics. It's a material they make out of petroleum—they can make it in a lot of consistencies. Very handy and cheap."

40

"Absolutely fascinating." Fortune stood and bounced on his heels. "Might I explore the neighborhood?"

"Well—maybe we should wait until daylight?" Linnea imagined the curtains twitching open as they walked past. Some of the stay-at-home moms on their street would probably have to invest in better flood insurance for the drool.

Kurt checked his phone. "Well—I've got a night shift starting, so I'll see you guys tomorrow afternoon. Feel free to use my bedroom, Ben." He gave a wave and jogged out the door.

Linnea and Fortune regarded one another. "Mr. Walton explained to me that he is your... roommate, is it? Not your employer. Or your *chère amie*."

"No. No, we're not... involved. Just friends." This was surreal—the conversation, the situation, all of it.

"He tells me you are his greatest friend in the world." Fortune's smile grew a bit melancholy. "I should give a very great deal to have someone say such a thing of me, and mean it the way your friend does."

Linnea found herself leaning unconsciously toward him. "But—what about your friends at the clubs? And from Eton and Oxford?"

Fortune shrugged. "Such friendships are often only as deep as a man's pockets."

"I'm sorry." She didn't know what else to say.

He grinned, revealing dimples. "You needn't be—it is only the way of things. But I am glad to know such things have changed. And, indeed, that such friendships transcend sex and color. I am a fierce Abolitionist, you see."

"Really?" She sat up straighter at that. "The book never mentioned—I mean, I didn't expect that."

Winged black brows—honestly, actually winged in shape, giving those dark eyes an otherworldly air, as though the owner was about to take flight in some no doubt classically graceful way—rose as they regarded Linnea, making her skin prickle. "Book? To what book do you refer? And why should you be surprised—because I am of means and yet wish to free my brethren? If I cannot make a living without standing on the backs of my fellow men, then perhaps I do not deserve to have said living."

"Very true," she answered, raising her hands in surrender and hoping he would forget about her slip. "Prejudice against people of color is considered unacceptable in our culture, so I'm glad you feel that way."

"I am delighted to hear it." He looked around the room. "Tell me of some of these devices, please. It is clear they have some function, but I cannot fathom what they might be. Is that," he indicated a large black screen on the wall, "some kind of picture frame?"

"Sort of!" she said brightly, picking up the remote control. "Watch—it's like having a theater in your living room." She turned it on.

His black eyes went wide. "What is it—what is happening? Some sort of game?"

42

"Yeah, it's college basketball. They do fictional dramas, too." She turned the channel. "Here—this one's a mystery show."

"A mystery… show? So these are actors, upon a stage? It looks so very real."

"Yep, actors reciting lines. All fake."

Fortune was frowning. "And how do we follow—now we are upon this man's face and now the other man has placed that item in his pocket. Oh!" Ben pressed a finger to his lips. "We should be silent, so that he may discover the partially burnt letter in the other man's pocket!" he whispered. "My apologies to the actors for my outburst."

She chuckled. "He can't hear you. It's just an image made of colored light. There's a device called a camera that captures the image and the sound. So they capture the actors' performance from all kinds of perspectives to make it more interesting."

He peered closely at the screen. "So the performers are at a distance, and transmitted through a series of lenses, like a telescope? But then the sound—how is it made loud enough for us to hear?"

"It isn't transmitted through lenses, though that's a good guess." She explained the workings of the TV to him as well as she was able—which, not being a physics major, wasn't all that well.

He was far smarter than she had expected. Not that she had thought he was stupid, of course. But he was catching on very quickly, laughing with delight at every new thing she explained to him. "Show me more,

Miss Santiago! Show me more of this wondrous world of yours!"

She suddenly found herself laughing along. "Come on—I'll show you the kitchen. You hungry?"

He rubbed his lean belly. "I've missed my dinner—I hope I have not caused you to do the same. If you had some cheese or bread, I could perhaps produce a passable ploughman's." He hesitated. "It would not be seemly for me to ask you to do so," he added quietly. "Though I had initially thought your role might be that of housekeeper to Mr. Walton when he asked you to fetch towels for me, he made it immediately clear that you are equals in every way."

"Oh." That construction on the situation hadn't even occurred to Linnea. "Yeah, most people don't have servants anymore. But I'd be glad to pull something together for you, since you're a guest! We've got... well, I don't want to subject you to reheated pizza. Or peanut butter and jelly. Um... I've got some frozen lasagna we could heat up?"

"I shall follow your lead in all things since I do not... well, I do know what jelly is. So Mr. Walton studies medicine, he tells me," Fortune went on as she retrieved the lasagna. "What is it you do, if I may be so bold as to ask?"

"Oh, I'm also a graduate student. Only not in medicine. I study history, and I have an assistantship to pay the bills."

Those fascinating brows of his went up again. "I confess myself surprised, though I suppose I should not be."

"By what?"

"In my day," he began, then laughed ruefully. "I sound the veriest graybeard. In any case, it is only that such intellectual pursuits were closed to women."

"Yes, women's rights are very much expanded in our time. We're considered the equals of men, mostly."

"And yet I could point to woman after woman whom I would consider man's superior," he replied with a sweet smile. The microwave dinged; Fortune jumped a bit.

"Yeah, so this is a microwave. It heats up food." Linnea pulled out the plastic carton of lasagna, put it on a plate and placed it on the table with a fork and a glass of water. "Eat up!" She took the chair across from him.

He sat and eyed it with some skepticism, but took a bite. "Hot!" he managed, waving his hand in front of his mouth.

"Oh, sorry! Should have warned you." She winced in sympathy.

Ben sipped at the water. "Some kind of Italian food?" he guessed.

"Yep. Lasagna."

"It has an interesting flavor," he commented, blowing carefully on the next bite.

Linnea wondered if he was just being nice. It was, after all, a microwavable TV dinner. Maybe she should... No, her cooking—with a few notable exceptions—would certainly be worse than anything out of a cardboard box. Every era had its cross to bear: the eighteenth century had cholera; the twenty-first had Linnea's lack of culinary skill.

"So you study history? What period, if I may be so bold?"

"Eighteenth century, actually." She smiled at him. It was almost impossible not to, with a face like that...!

Which at the moment was reflecting chagrin. "So... my period."

"Yeah. Something wrong with that?"

"Not in the least—I am just unaccustomed to being thought of as history. Is that why you brought me here, to ask about my time period?"

"N-no," she returned sheepishly. "I would love to pick your brains sometime, though." He looked startled and a little horrified. She burst out laughing. "It's a metaphor! I just meant, ask you questions and learn from you."

"Oh!" Fortune grinned. "Yes, that you may certainly do, though I cannot stay long."

"Right." How was she going to deal with that one? "We'll... send you back as soon as we can." Which was true, although how soon that might be, no one could tell.

"Thank you. I have responsibilities I must attend to, as diverting as this is." He rose from the table and glanced around. "Where is—? Oh. Er... can I help you clean these dishes?"

"Oh, here. We rinse out the plastic, and then it goes in the recycle... and the glass and fork go in the automatic dishwasher. Presto!"

He repeated everything she said, even the 'presto!' at the end, and followed it with an enormous yawn. "Forgive me! All of this... mysterious travel seems to have wearied me."

"Not at all. Why don't you get some sleep—here, I'll show you how the light switch works."

Soon enough, Linnea was able to head back to her bedroom. She dropped onto the edge of the bed, as exhausted as Fortune.

The most insane part of this evening wasn't, she realized, the fact that she had accidentally found a magical spell and brought a non-existent person from fictional Regency England to the modern world. Which was pretty darned insane, but it had inarguably happened, so there was little point in refusing to accept it. That aside, the strangest part was how different he was from what she'd expected.

Fortune's Folly had painted Ben Fortune as gorgeous—which he was, no question—and rich and courteous and well-dressed, athletic and fashionable. But it had said nothing whatsoever about his intelligence. He was amazingly quick, and greeted the modern world with enthusiasm.

In Belinda Burnworth's writing, Ben Fortune was somewhat charming at his first meeting with Araminta, but very reserved after that—Darcy-ish. He was never anything but scrupulously polite, but he very often seemed bored by everything and everyone except Araminta, and he was trying strenuously to deny his feelings for her.

Linnea pulled up one of her favorite *Fortune's Folly* fanfictions on her phone. It was one in which in a modern girl found herself transported into the novel and replaced Araminta in Ben Fortune's affections. He was almost disdainful of her at first, and somewhat cold.

But this Ben Fortune wasn't anything like either the book or the fanfictions, and Linnea was having trouble reconciling his boyish enthusiasm and excitement at the marvels of the modern world with his drawing-room boredom. He had told her he had no close friends—was he just bored by Regency high society in general?

The strength of Susan's dissertation topic struck her all over again. If only part of *Fortune's Folly* had been told from his point of view! All of this might have been explained.

But it had been a long day, and just as Linnea had strongly recommended that Ben get a good night's sleep, she intended to do the same. She would put on her comfiest PJs, put on some soothing music—Nora Jones, maybe—and turn in early.

Chapter Four

She was still awake at 7 AM when Susan messaged her on Faceplace, the phone dinging as Linnea read yet another piece of *Fortune's Folly* fanfiction. She had discovered that there were over a dozen fics on *FictionFan.net* alone in which a modern girl went to Regency England and seduced Ben Fortune, and even a few in which he came to the modern world. Not a one of them featured a Ben Fortune that in any way resembled the one currently sleeping in Kurt's bedroom.

WAKE UP! the texts said in all caps, as though the case of the letter would actually affect the volume of the text alert. *LINNEA, CHECK YOUR FORTUNE'S FOLLY!*

What? she typed back.

Do it. Now. Check the scene where she twists her ankle! I'm serious!

Frowning, Linnea pulled out her copy and flipped open to the scene. Araminta met Ben Fortune on his walk, she was injured, he carried her back to her Aunt Virulea's house...

Yeah? What about it? she texted.

What happens after the footman unlocks the conservatory?

Um... Fortune carries her inside?

Yeah? You read that part, and let me know when you have.

What was she on about? Sighing, Linnea flipped forward to that part of the scene.

Fortune set Araminta gently down upon the paving stone, it read. He pounded upon the door. "Ho! The house! Help for Miss Cavanaugh!"

Araminta wrapped her thin shawl more tightly about herself, her white walking gown dripping with the rain. Her ankle appeared swollen already.

There was a sound of footsteps inside, and then John the footman opened the door. "Miss?" he said, sounding surprised. "But I thought I heard a man's voice!"

Araminta looked up. "What do you—?" But it was clear to her what he meant. Mr. Fortune, who an instant before had been standing beside her on the paving stone, had vanished like a wraith into the rain.

Linnea nearly dropped the book. "Oh, no," she whispered. "Oh, shit!"

She read on, frantically. No Fortune. Araminta got up by herself (what had happened to the sprained ankle, Linnea wondered briefly?), rather put out that Fortune had left her at the door... Linnea flipped forward several pages. There was a card party, one that Linnea *knew* Fortune had attended, and he wasn't there! The guests commented on his absence. Apparently, he had disappeared whilst on a walk in the direction of Aunt Virulea's country house... There was talk of highwaymen, and Fortune's servants were on the verge of calling in the local militia. Oh, shit. This was terrible.

Found it, didn't you?

WHAT HAPPENED TO IT? Linnea texted back. But she already knew, she realized with a sinking feeling. She knew exactly where Ben Fortune had disappeared to: her living room.

Thing is, it's happening to every copy: published, digital... Ben Fortune's disappeared from his own book. And the rest of it is changing. And nobody knows how. After a minute, the text went on. *Some of us are trying to do something about it to preserve what we remember. I know you're busy, but—can you help?*

Linnea took a few deep breaths. It was stupid to try to bring somebody in on this, but... Susan would understand better than anyone else—wouldn't she? Kurt wasn't here, and Linnea needed to go to the archive to try to fix this mess, so somebody needed to watch Fortune...

It was stupid, and she knew it was stupid, but she wanted to have somebody to talk this through with. She

51

messaged Susan: *Sure. And actually, I really need your help with something too. Can you come over?*, added her address, and hit "send" before she could think better of it.

Her doorbell rang about a quarter of an hour later. Linnea hurried out to the living room and pulled the door open, realizing as she did so that she hadn't showered or changed her clothes from the night before.

Susan's expression went from cheerful to doubtful as she took in Linnea's appearance. "Something wrong?"

"Yeah. Um... come on in." How in the hell was she going to explain this without sounding completely insane? She had approximately five seconds to figure it out, because Susan looked like she was going to bolt. "So, the crazy thing with *Fortune's Folly*. Um... I think it might be my fault?"

"You mean the... the way the story's changing? How? It's not even *possible*, or it shouldn't be." Susan backed away a step, her gaze wary. "I guess some crazy hacker program could change the digital versions, but... you're saying you figured out a way to change the written word? I don't... how would you do that? *Why* would you do that?"

"I didn't do it on purpose! And a hacker program couldn't change hardcopy books," Linnea pointed out.

"Okay, thanks for the clarification. How 'bout we skip to the point, because frankly you're weirding me out."

"Well, I'm afraid the point is going to weird you out more," Linnea said, feeling very small. "Um... I accidentally brought Ben Fortune out of the book?"

There was a long pause, and then Susan picked up her purse. "Okay, cool, this has been fun, but I have to go—got some stuff going on with half the subject of my dissertation mysteriously disappearing overnight, so... I'll call you, okay?"

"Okay," Linnea said very quietly.

The door to Kurt's bedroom opened. "Forgive me for sleeping so late, Miss Santiago," Fortune said in a morning baritone that ought to have had a stick attached so Linnea could lick it like a lollipop. He was wearing the pajamas Linnea had found for him in Kurt's closet the night before. "I was wondering what the customs of this time were for breaking my fast—my stomach, I fear, is putting up quite a protest, and—" He noticed a gobsmacked Susan for the first time. "Do forgive my dreadful state of dress, madam. My own clothes were a trifle soaked." He bowed. "Ben Fortune, your servant."

"Shut the front door," said Susan, her eyes wide.

Ben glanced at it. "But—it *is* shut?"

Linnea looked at Susan hopefully. "Mr. Fortune," she said, her tone a little brighter, "this is Miss Susan Hu."

"Delighted, Miss Hu." He bowed again; while he was bent double Susan mimed a full body scream at Linnea, complete with clawing out her own eyes, though by the time he stood again she was her usual composed self.

"Brunch?" Susan said casually, all things considered. "Why don't you go get dressed and we'll go grab something to eat."

His smile was both sweet and apologetic. "I'm afraid I have only these borrowed sleep-clothes to wear, as my own are still rather damp."

"I'll help you find some street clothes, and then we'll go to a restaurant to brunch," Linnea answered, whipping quickly into Kurt's room to rummage something appropriate from the closet. "Let me know if those don't fit. And—uh—don't forget to brush your teeth," she added, blushingly repeating the directions she had heard Kurt give him the night before. She dashed out of his room again and shut the door behind her, facing Susan.

"Thank you, Miss Santiago," came faintly from behind the door as Susan regarded Linnea.

"I don't even know where to begin," Susan said in an undertone. "If it hadn't been for the weirdness with him disappearing from the books I'd say you've got yourself one hell of a cosplayer, there. But other things being equal..." She folded her arms across her chest. "You did. You pulled Ben Fortune... 'out of the everywhere into the here'." This concise statement was followed by a whispered list of profane words generally reserved for people in the extremis of astonishment.

"I know, right??" Linnea whispered furiously. "One thing I have to warn you, though: he doesn't know yet that he's fictional. Or was, until last night. We told him we accidentally pulled him into the future, but not that we pulled him out of a book. So don't mention anything about it—I think finding out that you're fictional would be a pretty tough pill to swallow."

"Oh, *that's* your tipping point, is it?" Susan practically laughed. "Yeah, okay, I see your point. And by the way, Belinda Burnworth, God rest her soul, could've used some help in the descriptive department. *That* guy is—is—" She shook her head. "Can't blame her, I guess, I haven't got the words either. And I usually prefer girls."

"I *know*!" Linnea was in full fangirl mode for the first time since this debacle began, and it was making her feel so much better about this ridiculousness.

Susan took her by the upper arms and gave her a shake. "Now listen, Linnea, I know we've only been friends since about 4:36 yesterday afternoon, according to Faceplace, but I am going to tell you something no other friend would tell you. Call it true friendship, call it selflessness, call it what you will, but here it is: you were wearing that outfit yesterday and obviously all night, and while I'm sure Mr. Fortune is used to some pretty ripe young maidens, I don't think you really want your impression upon him to be that you're making his eyes water a bit. Go, shower, put on something cute, make your hair adorable. Give that Araminta a run for her guinea-gold money. Do it for the rest of us who'll never get a chance. Go, Linnea! Go!"

Feeling like an Olympic athlete, Linnea dashed out of the room and turned on the shower.

She soaped up as thoroughly and as quickly as possible and towel-dried her hair, then hurried to her room to find the perfect outfit.

This was nearly impossible. She wanted to look nice, but not too dressy for the local cafe and university library. She wanted to look her best, but not totally scandalize a Regency gentleman. There were no options in this Venn diagram of fail.

At last she shrugged her shoulders and put on what she would wear to a coffee date with a cute guy she'd met online: her best jeans, ankle-high boots, a cute, dressy little shirt in a shade of green that showed off her complexion and her hair to perfection, a little jewelry, a dash of makeup (okay, she took too long over the makeup, but it was time well spent on getting that subtle look). At last she emerged, resplendent, into the light of the living room. "Ready to go?" she asked nonchalantly.

The smile on Ben Fortune's face as he jumped to his feet was worth it. "I have waited far longer with far less delightful results," he said gallantly. "Miss Santiago, Miss Hu, I do not do you justice, but am honored to escort you nonetheless." His cheeks flushed. "I fear I have not the wherewithal to remunerate Mr. Walton for his very kind loan to me last eve, and I do not fully understand your system of currency, but I trust you will show me what is appropriate?"

"Loan? Oh, he gave you some cash. Yeah, don't worry about it." Linnea looked at Susan. "You want to walk to the cafe? It's only a few blocks." And she didn't want to terrify Fortune with the car just yet.

"Sure. Let's go."

They stepped out onto the street, both Susan and Linnea watching Fortune with anticipation. His eyes, dark as soot with a mischievous cast to them, went completely round at the sight of the streets and the houses and the cars, the signs and the traffic signals, the baby strollers and dogs on leashes, and...

"How *clean* it all smells," was his first observation. "There is all this humanity and civilization and yet the air is fresh and does not... does not *encase* one."

"Like in London, you mean?"

"Yes, in the streets where one must constantly guard against the call of a maid doing her day's cleaning, or watch one's step lest one take a horse's calling card into an establishment upon one's boot." He smiled. "I trust you will warn me of similar risks here." Ben lifted that aristocratic nose to the air. "What is that scent of— is it burning? Yet is it not fire."

"You're probably smelling the cars. See?" Linnea pointed to a busier road as they reached an intersection. "Horseless carriages! They run on an internal combustion engine that burns refined petroleum."

He stared at her for a moment, then began to laugh good-naturedly. "I understood not one word after 'they run on'. Will you explain over our meal?" He gave her a happy smile and then pointed to a neon sign of dancing bacon and eggs, proclaiming, 'The Three Muskeggteers'. "Is that the establishment we shall be attending?"

Susan nodded, pushing her sleek hair behind one ear. "Don't let the sign fool you. The food here is great."

Ben shrugged. "I rather like the sign."

Chuckling, they led him into the restaurant.

The decor was in a fifties diner style, and they requested a booth, Ben sliding in beside Linnea. She ordered her own drink, and then a water with lemon and a soda for Ben. "This is cola," she said, indicating it when it came. "Don't drink it too fast at first: it's bubbly, like champagne."

He frowned. "Is it customary to imbibe in the morning? I should not like to be disguised so early in the day."

"Don't worry—it's not alcoholic," Linnea answered, grinning at his slang. "Just sugary."

"Oh." He took a sip, and then another. "It's like some kind of fizzy treacle drink."

She chuckled. "Yep, pretty much."

Breakfast foods hadn't changed that much since the eighteenth century, and Ben recognized most of the combinations of eggs, biscuits, sausage, ham, pancakes, and bacon on the menu. He was excited to see that there were omelets and crepes, but ended up ordering a very hearty brunch of ham, eggs, bacon, and toast. He was inordinately intrigued by something called 'scrapple' but both companions talked him out of it, and so he sat happily eating the meal placed before him.

Ben dipped his toast points into the poached egg yolk. "So, Miss Hu, will you tell me something of yourself?"

"I'm a graduate student, like Linnea. Only I'm studying literature instead of history."

His ears visibly pricked up. "What sort of literature?"

"British eighteenth century," she grinned.

Ben tilted his head. "Not Chinese literature of the period?"

She blinked at him for a moment, then took a deep breath as Linnea mentally face-palmed. "I actually don't read Chinese," Susan said very calmly. "My family has been in the United States for over a hundred years. Although I value my Chinese heritage, I'm very much an American."

Fortune went a deep red. "My very sincere apologies, Miss Hu. I intended no offense." It was clear enough he wasn't sure what he'd done, only that that he wished he hadn't done it.

"I know you didn't," she answered calmly. "But people often assume that east-Asian people can't be American—which is really quite foolish." She gave him a warm smile, as if to gently include him in the joke.

"Yes, of course it is. How idiotic of me." He cleared his throat. "I have met no one of your background before. It is a very great pleasure to know you—and very kind in you to forgive my foolish blunder."

She smiled again. "Not at all. So here you are— an eighteenth-century man—with two eighteenth-century scholars! What fun." She gave Linnea a mischievous side-eye.

"Shall I prepare to have my brains picked?" he asked with good humor.

"Actually, yes," she said, pulling a notebook and pen out of her purse. "I have a few questions to ask..."

It was more than a few, but at last Linnea suggested they go to the library. "I have to look up... some things related to time travel," she said, "which involves me going to the restricted area of the archives. Would you two care to come to campus with me?"

The others readily agreed, Ben proclaiming himself eager to see what university education looked like now. "I assume I shall see a broad sampling of humanity, and no robes nor caps, as you do not wear them. Shall I brace myself in some other way?"

"Just for the elevator," Linnea grinned.

Ben Fortune's first ride in a car was a memorable experience for all concerned, he was sure. Miss Santiago drove, which he initially found impressive, immediately followed by utterly terrifying once the vehicle got up to speed. He didn't *actually* scream, but he clenched his teeth so hard he was surprised he had any left by the time they came to a stop. There were convenient creases in the seat cushions where he could dig in his fingers in a desperate grip for dear life, which was surely a preferable alternative to climbing into Miss Hu's lap, not that he didn't consider it. However, the belt that buckled him in seemed to keep him safe enough: at any rate, they arrived alive, and he supposed that was what mattered.

"All right back there?" Miss Santiago asked lightly, as if to convey the idea that this was a normal occurrence, something he should get used to.

"I'll let you know when my stomach has arrived," he growled sourly in return, wrestling with his belt buckle. "I only hope my breakfast arrives with it."

"Well, if it doesn't, please don't barf it up all over my upholstery."

"I do not *barf*," he told her with dignity, inwardly swearing at his heaving insides.

"*Good.*"

The university campus was lovely, Ben thought, walking between the two women, his hands behind his back. Though a few of the buildings were unattractive and blocky, others were designed more in a classical style, and still others in the styles popular in his own day. The library, an imposing edifice, was one of these latter, and he inwardly admitted to some surprise at the size of the building. Surely this college must be on a par with those at Oxford...

Miss Hu had some things to do in her office, so she left them at the library doors. Miss Santiago picked up a leaflet from a counter and handed it to him.

"There's a map of the building in there," she told him. "I can't take unauthorized persons into the archive—are you going to be okay on your own?"

"Will I be what?" He raised a quizzical brow at her.

"All right," she translated.

"I assure you, Miss Santiago, I have visited libraries before. I am perfectly capable of amusing myself until you have finished whatever it is you must do."

She gave him that smile he had seen on her face several times before: sweet but impish. Her brandy-colored eyes twinkled. "All right, all right. I'll meet you here in a couple of hours." She left him to himself.

Ben began at the entrance hall of the imposing structure, which boasted a variety of bronze plaques in memoriam of various personages of import to the school. Centered in the floor was a large mosaic compass, and he amused himself by standing dead center and facing true north while he studied the map of the building.

History, he thought initially, and began to walk in the direction of that room, but his eye was caught by a rather elaborate artistic installation in bronze and marble: a tribute, he read, to the Spirit of Education, as represented by a young woman in the classical Grecian style of undress holding aloft a burning torch, and a quote from someone named William Butler Yeats. "*Education*," he read aloud, "*is not the filling of a pail, but the lighting of a fire*," and the sentiment made him smile. How very true, he thought, examining the statue with interest.

There was something of Miss Santiago in the character of that marble face, to his mind, though it was dead white, of course, nothing like the warm, golden-brown skin that made the living woman's features so appealing. But there was a dedication to be seen in the marble face, an unmistakable intelligence: though upon reflection, Miss Santiago's kind nature and good humor formed the greater part of her aspect, and he readily admitted that he found no small pleasure in looking at her. Even if she did drive like a madwoman.

Ben peered around the side of the statue, intrigued by the "everlasting flame" in the torch it held high. Contrarily, there was no discernible flame, though the candle certainly flickered with light. But no, the wick was dead. How on Earth was such a thing managed? Without thinking he reached out to touch it: it was not warm. It wasn't even particularly waxy. He looked about for a switch, similar to that he'd seen at Miss Santiago's abode, but no. And her... bulbs, yes, that was the term—the bulbs in her lamps were rounded, and had no wicks such as these.

Wary of being burnt, he gingerly poked at the wick; to his horror the candle promptly fell from its perch and rolled across the length of the hall. Ben ran after it, looking about to be sure no one had seen his inadvertent vandalism, and snatched it up, only to discover that the "everlasting flame" of Education had gone out.

A pair of chattering students came into the library and he put the candle behind his back and nodded pleasantly at them before pretending to be absorbed in the architecture of the ceiling while casually sidling back toward the statue. They paid him little notice and passed through the room without comment.

Ben heaved a breath of relief as they disappeared from sight and reached to replace the candle to its rightful place, whereupon the entire bronze torch detached itself from the statue's hand and plummeted to the ground with a loud and echoing clang. He cast a wild glance around, dropped the candle, and ran in the same direction the students had gone.

He found himself confronted by a broad vestibule centered with an odd-looking double staircase. It took him a moment to realize that the stairs themselves were moving: one set up, the other down. Ben looked about himself; there was no one to instruct him, and equally no one to observe him, so he approached the 'up' stairs warily. Each step was bordered with a yellow line; all one need do would be to step between them, he concluded, and reached out a foot. But the memory of his ride with Miss Santiago came to the fore and he snatched his leg back, only to stand there dithering.

He consulted the map. The History section, apparently, required that he go up this infernal device. Gathering his courage, he steeled himself to take a step beyond the yellow line. He was still hesitating when a voice said, "Excuse me—can I help you?"

Ben couldn't help the sigh of relief that escaped him. "Indeed, I should be grateful for some assistance, Mrs…?"

"Dr. Bialecki," she smiled, shaking his hand. She was older than Miss Santiago and Miss Hu, with a cloud of short, curly hair and lively brown eyes.

He only just checked himself from bowing, instead returning her smile. Apparently this was how it was done these days. "My pleasure," he returned politely. "Ben Fortune. I was hoping to find the—"

"Ben Fortune?" she exclaimed, surprisingly loud. "Oh, sorry. I just—were you named for the Burnworth character?"

He found himself completely unable to parse this question. "No, I don't believe so. I was named by my father, for reasons known best to him, I suppose. Could I trouble you to help me find the History section?"

"Of course. It's on the third floor." She pointed to his map. "Right there."

Chewing on his lip, he nodded. "I see, yes. And so if I take these—er—stairs here, will I find more such awaiting me above?"

"There's a set of regular stairs in the east stairwell. Or you could take the elevator—it's over there."

Ben glanced in the direction she was pointing but saw nothing that looked as though it might lead upward. He took a breath, squaring his shoulders. "These are right here," he observed, "and thus must be considered safe enough to use, I believe." He glanced at the stranger for confirmation.

She seemed to be suppressing a smile, but her gaze was kind. "Yes. Do you want to go up together?" she asked, holding out her elbow.

"I should be most grateful. I have never—that is to say, where I am from, we do not have such devices." Ben took her arm, but properly, tucking her hand into the crook of his elbow.

They stepped together beyond the yellow line, squarely onto one of the steps. Slowly they began to rise upward.

"Amazing," he muttered, smiling when she turned to look at him. "I shall have to become used to new experiences, I expect, while I am visiting." They were at the top of the moving stairs, and Dr. Bialecki exerted a slight pressure on his arm to urge him off of it at the right moment. He grinned at their joint triumph.

"What part of England are you from?" Dr. Bialecki asked, then added smilingly, "Rosebury-on-Wye?"

His brows lifted. "Why, exactly the place, indeed! Do you know it?"

"Er—no, I'm afraid not," she answered, with a somewhat strange expression. "Though I did visit Herefordshire, some years ago."

Ben's smile widened. "Excellent! And what were your thoughts? I hope it did not rain too often. It can be inclement there, though even the storms hold their own beauty."

"No, it was sunny the day we visited Leominster," she answered, though she appeared somewhat distracted. "We visited the home of Belinda Burnworth, the novelist."

"Leominster?" His brows drew together. "I am afraid I'm unfamiliar with the place. Or the lady," he added apologetically. He consulted his map and looked around. "The east stairwell would be...?"

"That way—why don't I just walk with you?" she suggested, nodding toward a door marked 'Stairs'. "What brings you to the States?"

"I am honoured," Ben told her politely, and they walked along together. "It was an... unexpected journey. Spur of the moment, as you might say. I am visiting friends for a short time," he enlarged, pleased to have come up with this very reasonable explanation.

"Are they students here, or just locals?"

"Graduate students, or at least Miss Santiago and Miss Hu are. Mr. Walton is a medical student. This seems a very fine college," Ben added diplomatically as they mounted the stairs. "Certainly for size upon a scale with any other I have seen."

"Miss Hu! This wouldn't by any chance be Susan Hu?"

"Yes, that is her given name. Are you acquainted?"

"I'm her adviser," she answered. "Oh—and here's the History section!"

This time he did bow, realizing only belatedly that he probably shouldn't have. "You have my gratitude, Dr. Bialecki, for delivering me safely. We shall meet again, perhaps. A very good day to you."

"And you," she answered in an odd tone and walked away, casting him another look over her shoulder as she went.

The open arch to the History section beckoned. To one side was a strange-looking, rectangular steel door: layered, as though to a vault or some such, and he wondered what treasures might be within. As if in answer to his mental inquiry, the door slid open with a bell-like sound, and... people tumbled out, seven or eight of them at least. Ben craned his neck for a glimpse into the vault and saw only a tiny, empty room. *But— what would all those people be doing in...?* —But the door slid closed again before he could finish the thought.

One of the young men who had disembarked, an unusual sort of close-fitting cap on his head with a bill in the back—*to protect his neck, perhaps, like a dustman?*—meandered over to a squarish receptacle by the History entrance and pushed open a small door at the top to deposit an empty bottle. Ben jumped nearly a foot when the receptacle replied, 'Thank you' in a cultured, feminine voice.

He waited until the small crowd had dispersed, then warily approached the receptacle and poked the little door.

"Thank you," it said.

"You're—er—very welcome," he muttered hurriedly, and the vault opposite opened again, expelling yet more people from the same tiny, empty room. Ben jammed his fingers into his hair—had the world gone mad around him?

A few daring souls entered the vault, and the door slid shut. Ben found himself staring at it as though mesmerized, waiting to see—to see what—and sure enough, in a few minutes the door slid open, but the people inside had utterly gone, and new ones stepped off. More magic? He didn't know, didn't want to know, and shouldered his way past a couple of people to get into the History section and the familiar comfort of books.

"Thank you," he heard the receptacle say behind him, and he moved a little faster.

Historians, he thought in disgust an hour or so later. He'd spent some time looking up his own period, and while it was correct in the main, there were several appalling oversights. Some important personages whom he knew personally were entirely missing from the record, and some other details just seemed off from what Ben himself knew was true. As to the maps, Rosebury-on-Wye was nowhere to be found, though there were many towns and cities of which he'd never heard, including the aforementioned Leominster. At the last he gave up and decided to apply his attentions elsewhere, where the unreliability of the information mightn't be such an irritant.

Ben was deep in a tome on the American Civil War when someone tapped him on the shoulder. He looked up.

Linnea was grinning at him. "How did I know to find you in the History section?" she teased.

Greatly relieved to see a familiar face after the travails of the morning, he smiled back. "I can only presume more magic, Miss Santiago. Have you concluded your business?"

"Yep, got the scans I need," she answered. "Come on—Susan said she'd meet us in the gardens." She led him back to the dinging metal doors. They opened, and she stepped into the small room.

Ben balked; he couldn't help it. "Where—um— where do we go?" he asked, trying not to sound utterly panicked.

"We're just going to take the elevator down to the ground floor," she said, and to his surprise, reached out and took his hand, pulling him into the small room with her.

He cleared his throat nervously as the door whirred shut. "Is not going down in an 'elevator' something of an oxymoron?" he asked, fidgeting. "We could perhaps have taken those moving stairs." At least that way he could see where he was.

There was a small lurch, then a noise, then another small lurch, a ding—and when the doors opened this time, the corridor in front of them was completely changed. Ben hurriedly stepped out, and then looked about in wonder, mouth agape as he tried to figure it out. Finally he turned to face Miss Santiago. "The room— the 'elevator'—it moves from floor to floor, as a dumbwaiter. Pulleys?"

"Yes, and an electric motor."

At last it made sense, and Ben laughed. "How very clever."

Miss Santiago smiled at his enthusiasm, and they made their way out of the building. On the way out through the vestibule, she pointed to the torch, lying on the floor by the statue. "Tsk. Undergrads." She rolled her eyes.

Ben opened his mouth to correct her, then decided discretion would be the better part of—well, perhaps not valor, in this case. But definitely a good idea.

The garden in the middle of South Green was a very pretty spot where Linnea had sometimes retreated to eat lunch during office hours. Susan wasn't there yet, so Linnea led Fortune to a bench.

He rubbed his hands together. "What is next in our plan?"

"Sadly, a lot of analyzing documents for me," Linnea said glumly.

"Is there nothing I can do to assist you in finding whatever it is you look for? I am not unfamiliar with methods of research. I should also like to learn all I can of your time before you send me back."

"Um, well you see, the thing is..." Linnea shifted uncomfortably. She had to tell him; she was just afraid of his response. "We didn't—*I* didn't bring you to the future on purpose. It was a total accident—I didn't even

realize that what I was using was a magical spell. And...
I don't actually know how to send you back."

"You—you don't—" He stared at her; she could
see the whites all around the coal-dark irises of his eyes.
"But—I *must* return! I have responsibilities—I have—"

"It's not—oh boy. Um... Here's the thing, Mr.
Fortune," Linnea said slowly. "It's not so much that I
brought you forward in time." Those magnificent dark
brows of his came together. "It's—we brought you out
of a novel."

"I *beg* your—" He stood up, all dignity, even in
Kurt's castoff jeans. "I fail to see the sport in this—to
wrest me from my home, my world, my loved ones—
and now to try to tell me that none of it *exists*?" Those
dark eyes were utterly stricken. "I had believed you a
different kind of woman, Miss Santiago—had imbued
you with virtues which I now see were the product of
my own imagination. It is a passing strange kind of
cruelty you inflict upon me for your amusement." His
chin firmed, and he refused to look at her.

"No—no wait, Mr. Fortune," Linnea said,
jumping up and taking his arm. "I'm not teasing you.
I'm serious. Here." Linnea had stuck the novel in her
purse that morning. She pulled it out. "See? *Fortune's
Folly*, by Belinda Burnworth. Now listen." She flipped
it open and read the passage where he first met Araminta
in the conservatory. "'Good to know the name of one's
savioress, I find,'" she read. "'It's coming down
sideways out there. Does it often blow up suddenly like
this?'"

72

He had frozen. "But that is almost exactly as it happened!" Fortune snatched the book from her hand and reread the passage. Linnea waited, watching his face go white. He sat back down, hard. "Is—is my fate in here? Is it all foretold?"

"No—I don't think so," Linnea answered. "I mean, it's changed already. Originally you appeared in the book right through to the end. Now, since I brought you out, you suddenly disappear from the plot halfway through. The book changed. So the events in the book aren't written in stone."

Susan approached as Fortune ran his fingers through his hair. "I must get back, I must—if I am not there, who can say what will happen to her?" He turned wide, dark eyes on her. "You must help me—you must help me return!"

"Of course," Linnea said, putting her hand on his arm and glancing up at Susan, who raised her eyebrows at the tableau. "I'm going to search through the papers until I find the right spell," she promised, knowing even as she said it that she might never get through all the papers, and that the spell might not exist. But she was certainly going to try. "We'll get you back to her. And maybe this time you'll decide to be honest with her about your feelings."

"Decide to be—to whom do you refer? I assure you, I have hid my true feelings from no one, except where rudeness forbids."

Linnea all but rolled her eyes. He was being coy. Typical Fortune.

"It's all right, we know," Susan said gently. "You don't have to hide it from us. You're in love."

He could not have looked more astonished if she'd pulled a salmon from behind her back and smacked him across the face with it. "I assure you, Miss Hu, I am heart-whole. I believe I would know better than you."

"No, really," Linnea added. "We know all about Araminta."

"Ara—" His rather patrician nose actually wrinkled. "Araminta *Cavanaugh*? You cannot mean her."

"Yes," Linnea insisted. "We know you're in love with Araminta Cavanaugh."

He stared at them. "But—I *detest* the silly girl!"

Chapter Five

"You aren't in love with Araminta?" Susan said, her eyes wide.

Fortune stared at them for a long moment. "No—no, it is too much. Impossibility after impossibility have I swallowed at your behest but this— this is too much." He let out a bitter laugh. "I? In love with that clinging, insipid, vain, foolish, ovine, odiferous—to say nothing of the horror of her connexions! Were she the veriest paragon, her gorgon of an aunt Vitupera would be enough to drive any man of sanity away. No." He shook his sable head. "You go too far, ladies. I will believe all else you say before that. But that I must *love* Araminta Cavanaugh? That is entirely beyond the pale." Ben got up and began to pace, hands behind his back.

Linnea laughed suddenly, then covered her mouth with her hands in chagrin. He gave her a haughty look. "As usual, I fail to see the humor, Miss Santiago."

She descended into giggles. "All these fangirls, all over the world, squeeing over your love story for centuries, and actually, you think Araminta's 'ovine and odiferous'!" She started laughing all over again. Even Susan was grinning.

His lips quirked. "'Squeeing'?"

"Like this. EEEEEEEEEEEEEEEE!!!!!!!" Linnea did a full-body squee, kicking her legs and waving her arms back and forth spasmodically.

Fortune clapped his hands over his ears. "They don't really?"

"Oh, they do," Susan chimed in. "And they'd be squeeing even more loudly if they knew you didn't like Araminta after all and were... *available*."

Linnea almost collapsed laughing. "Oh my God, we're in a fanfiction come true!"

"A fan—" Fortune shook his head, but he was now smiling wryly. "If I stop to ask the meaning of each term we shall be here all day. As to Miss Cavanaugh, I have it on good authority that her pomade is a home receipt of lanolin and tarragon, giving her hair a slightly greenish tint and smelling like nothing so much as an old mutton stew. I have heard her hair referred to as 'guinea-gold'. I take leave to inform you that guineas are not as yellow as one might presume, especially after good usage. Also her front teeth protrude, thusly." He used his fingers to demonstrate. "Though her appearance would count for little if she were not such a... a *noodle*. Never has she a thought of her own but that her aunt—or the latest overwrought romantic novel—has planted it in her mind. I would sooner love..." He cast about. "I would sooner love this bench, for it at least combines an attractive form with useful function. Are you yet convinced?" The two women nodded, nearly stifled with laughter, Linnea wiping at her eyes. "I shall take that as an affirmative. To my present situation: Araminta Cavanaugh's matrimonial machinations aside, fictional or not, I *must* return!" His expression darkened as he said it.

Susan rubbed between her brows. "Hold up a minute, though. You said, just now, 'What will happen to her if I am not there?' You obviously don't mean Araminta—are you in love with someone else, is that the mystery?" She tilted her head. "I'm confused. Who did you mean?"

"My sister, Sophia."

Linnea sat up. "Wait—sister?"

"Oh, yeah, remember? She's at school in Bath, isn't she? She only gets mentioned once in the book," Susan told them.

Ben nodded dolefully. "She is indeed at school in Bath, for another two years before her coming out at eighteen. But if I am not there, apart from the grief I fear she will suffer—is suffering—her guardianship reverts to an uncle who has little reason to love her and a poor reputation. Heavens above, what am I to do?" His fingers were in his hair again, his head bowed.

Linnea had stopped laughing in the face of his obvious distress. She rose and put her hand on his back, hoping he wouldn't be offended at the gesture. "I'm so sorry, Mr. Fortune," she said softly.

Susan laid her hand on his shoulder. "We'll do everything we can to help. We got you here; we can get you back." Linnea gave her friend a grateful smile at her taking part of the responsibility for a mistake she hadn't even been present for.

He lifted his head after a moment, offering Linnea the merest breath of a smile. "Thank you. I am sorry for my earlier assumption, Miss Santiago. I ought to have known you would not torment me in such a way. Mr. Walton's assessment of your character would seem to be correct. I am at your entire mercy, but I… I believe you will try to help me."

Relieved, Linnea patted his shoulder gently. "Well, you've got two eighteenth-century scholars on the case now. We'll figure it out."

"Oh! Speaking of scholars…" Susan broke in. "I take it you met my adviser in the library?"

"Yes—Dr. Bialecki, was it? She very kindly helped me to find the History section," Ben acknowledged. "How did you know?"

"She hunted me down in the office. Wanted to know all about this guy who called himself Ben Fortune. She asked how we had met, and I said on an online fansite for *Fortune's Folly*."

"Oh, that was a good move!" Linnea applauded.

"'Online fansite'?" Ben was frowning, dark brows drawn together. "And what is that?"

"It's—a way for people who enjoy the book to contact one another and talk about it," Linnea explained.

"Oh." He subsided, still frowning.

"I don't think she bought it, though," Susan added. "She gave me a really funny look."

Ben looked a little confused: he mouthed, *"Bought it?"*

"Wasn't convinced by it." Linnea blew out her cheeks. "Well, there's nothing we can do about it now. Come on, let's go back to the apartment and get to work."

They stopped at a local department store on the way back home to grab a few things for Fortune so that he didn't have to keep raiding Kurt's supplies, and dropped his own clothes off at a drycleaners, not without reservations on Linnea's part as to whether they'd hold together through the process. Fortune had seemed to relax about the car rides, thank goodness.

As they loaded bags into the trunk of Linnea's car, Susan confronted their visitor. "Listen, I keep meaning to bring up an important social point for this time period, but I keep forgetting. Generally speaking, people of equal social standing use first names. You'd call me Susan—though not Sue unless you don't want to keep your teeth. You'd call Linnea by her name, and Kurt, and so forth. And if it's all right, we'd call you Ben. Or Benjamin, or whatever."

"Not Benjamin," he said quickly. "My name is not—it's Ben. And you are most welcome to use it, Susan."

"Okay, first of all, why not Sue?" Linnea wanted to know as they all climbed into the car—Susan in the front, now that Ben seemed to require less soothing.

"Because then my name becomes Susie Sue Hu who is no more than two," Susan said darkly.

Linnea thought about that. "A sore point, obviously. Susan it is. And secondly, what *is* Ben short for?"

Ben was silent for a long time. "My given name was Benoni. I don't use it."

Linnea bit her lips. Susan smiled faintly. "I can see why."

He gave a ghost of a smile. "It is a bit of a comical name. My father had his reasons, I suppose."

"The fact that you didn't murder him is proof of your filial piety," Susan nodded sagely.

"You'd better let your girlfriend know where you are," Linnea suddenly told her. "Do you have classes to get to?"

Susan took out her phone and consulted it. "Timely warnings all. Unfortunately, I do have some work to do, so I've got to bail pretty soon." She began texting.

"If you will excuse my constant ignorance, ladies," Ben interjected from the back seat, "what is that device you are using? Some sort of instant communication instrument?"

"Yeah—it's called a phone," Linnea explained as they pulled up in front of her apartment. "You can talk to people even if they're halfway around the world, and you can send them written messages. ...Thanks again, Susan," she added as her new friend unlocked her car.

Susan gave a wave. "I'll be in touch, or you will. Don't do anything cool without me."

Linnea laughed—she couldn't help it. "Sure thing."

Ben helped her carry things into the apartment. "The use of the word 'cool', from the context in which I've now heard you use it several times... it means 'all right, interesting, fascinating,' or merely an affirmative, is that right? Like that other word—okay?"

"Wow, you're quick," Linnea smiled.

"So my schoolmasters said, and a good thing, too, for they were ready with switches should I play the dunce," he told her. "It's one of the few things my father took pride in." He hesitated for a moment. "Mi—er, Linnea—may I see the novel, please?"

She hesitated for a moment, then pulled it out of her bag. "It's changed, you know. Now that you're not there anymore—the novel is different. I haven't read the new version yet."

Ben nodded. "So I gather, which is why I should very much like to borrow it, if you do not mind. I should like to know what happened to my sister." His expression was sober indeed.

"Of course." She handed it to him. "You'll have to tell me what happens." Kurt's bedroom door was closed, which meant he was likely asleep after his long shift, so she didn't want to disturb him by going in to put away Ben's clothes. "I think I'm going to go ahead and get some research done: no time like the present!" Linnea dropped onto the couch and pulled out the scans of the commonplace book.

They had been reading side by side for nearly an hour when Kurt suddenly emerged from his bedroom. "Lin?" His voice seemed oddly strained. "Can I see you for a sec?"

"What now?" she muttered worriedly, and got up to talk to him. Kurt beckoned her into he bedroom and closed the door carefully behind her. "What is it?" she asked.

He rubbed the back of his neck. "Word's out— it's all over the news. You're gonna have to tell him that he came out of a book, that he's not..." Kurt shook his head. "I was gonna say real, but that's not right. That he used to be fictional, I guess."

"Oh. Yeah. Susan and I already told him. Why?"

"Did you?" Her friend's brows rose. "How'd he take it?"

"I think he's still processing. It's... a lot to take in."

Kurt nodded slowly. "Yeah. It would be. Poor guy."

It was Linnea's turn to frown. "What did you see on the news?"

He picked up his laptop. "Just that the story's gotten BIG. Here—I'll show you both." They went back to the living room and Kurt cued up a video on a major news website. He set the laptop on the coffee table in front of them and hit 'play.'

On the screen a breathless newscaster described the mysterious changes to every copy of *Fortune's Folly*; behind her was an enlarged promo photo of Tom

Hattleson, looking bravely into the distance, the moors behind him. "The production company says the parts of the movie that have been filmed and the script are still intact," Kurt told them, "but in every damn book, he's just... gone." He gave Ben's shoulder a brief squeeze.

"Yeah," Linnea said quietly, "that's what Susan told us."

"It's why it is most imperative that I return as soon as—*who* is that gentleman in the background?" broke in Ben.

"Huh? Oh, that's you," Kurt replied. "Shh."

"It most certainly is *not* me—"

"Shhh," returned Kurt. "I want to hear the rest of this."

"I just can't believe he's gone!" a teenage girl sobbed. Another one was shrugging. "We're still getting the movie. So it's not like the story's disappeared."

Linnea scoffed audibly.

"It's not the same," another girl broke in mournfully. "They always leave out so much in the movie... It's not the same."

The newscaster returned. "No one seems to have any explanation about how such widespread vandalism was accomplished, or why."

The image changed to a pair of scientists. They looked at one another, then at the camera, and shrugged. "We have not yet come up with any theory as to how this was accomplished," one of them said.

"But among the general public, theories abound," insisted the newscaster.

83

"It's the aliens," one young man said, hair all on end. He was wearing a green t-shirt that read "I BELIEVE." There were a large number of people behind him, apparently having a party and waving signs at the sky. An enthusiastic partier waved at the camera, his shirt reading "I've been PROBED!" "This is the first major sign of their presence," the interviewee went on. "Soon they'll take the faithful with them away to the sky, and *I'm* going to be on that ship!"

The shot changed to another background. "That's nonsense," a different man opined. "Clearly, the government is testing new technology they have not released to the public yet." He nodded sapiently.

"There is no way to choose between the theories," the reporter concluded. "The only clue is that it seems to have confined itself to the written word, thus far. But who knows how long—or if—that boundary will last."

"Oh my God," Linnea groaned, pressing her palms to her cheeks. "This is a *disaster*."

"Conspiracy theorists crawling out of the woodwork," Kurt agreed. "Personally I subscribe to the idea that aliens, with their superior technology, would choose an eighteenth-century chick-lit book to mess with as an opening parlay."

Linnea gave a little chuckle in spite of herself. "Stop calling it chick-lit, you chauvinist!"

Her roommate made a face at her and shrugged. "'Swhat it is." He looked over at Fortune. "How you holding up, bud? Settling in all right?"

84

Ben seemed to take a moment to parse the questions, then nodded. "Miss San—I should say Linnea—has been most careful to look after me." He reddened and looked as though he might add something more, but did not.

"Cool, cool," was Kurt's reply. "I see you got some clothes and stuff—let me clear you out a drawer. We'll keep splitting the room, if that's okay—you can have the bed when I'm on night shift and the couch when I'm home. Fair?"

"More than generous," Ben allowed. "Thank you, Mr.—er—Kurt."

Linnea glanced at her phone. "Well, I think it's probably about time for dinner."

Ben looked toward the kitchen expectantly, but Kurt pulled up a menu on his laptop. "I'm in the mood for some tikka masala, myself. Anybody else?"

"Um—I might heat up a frozen pizza," Linnea answered. With Ben to think about, she really needed to watch her pennies now, even more than before.

"What about you, Ben? My treat," said Kurt expansively. "You like Indian food?"

"Oh yes, curries and pilaus were quite popular in my time," he answered complacently.

"Then we are going to get along just fine. I recommend the chicken korma for the newbie." Kurt nudged him with a grin and entered the order, closing up the computer. "Okay. I'm going to put in a load of laundry while we wait for the food." He disappeared into his room.

Left with each other, Ben smiled down at Linnea. She smiled back a little. "Guess I'd better go preheat the oven."

He hesitated for a moment, then followed her. "We did much the same in my time," he told her conversationally. "It required building a hot fire and then scraping out the coals. That," he nodded at the buttons on the oven, "looks much easier."

She chuckled. "Definitely." She checked the box on the pizza and then pressed a couple of buttons.

"I would share my chicken korma with you, if you liked," Ben offered. "You seem unenthusiastic about your own meal. Perhaps I should not have been so ready to accept Kurt's generosity again," he added, brows drawn. "It is hard to know what's acceptable, in this world."

"Oh, he wouldn't have offered if he hadn't meant it," she assured him with a smile.

"Nonetheless I must find a way to pay him back—to pay you both back for your generosity." He fell into a brown study, sitting at the kitchen table.

"Ben, don't worry about it," she said gently, sitting down beside him. "We're here to help you. Isn't that what friends are for?"

His gaze settled on her face, and for the first time she could see that his irises were actually a very dark brown, like the walnut ink Janky had preferred to use. His lips curved. "I have never met a woman like you, Linnea Santiago: strong, competent, clever, kind, the equal of any man I know. Women like you are not so common in my world, and it is much the poorer for it."

Oh, Lord. If he kept smiling at her like that, she was going to pull an Araminta and swoon. "Thank you," she managed faintly.

That smile went mischievous. "And you do not smell of old mutton stew, for which I am devoutly thankful."

Kurt came out of his room, arms full of clothes. "We need any towels or anything?" he asked Linnea.

"Um... no," she said uncertainly, still looking at Ben. Kurt headed in the direction of the utilities room.

"Ben—" Linnea hesitated. "How are you feeling? About the news that you're fictional?"

He grew thoughtful, his gaze clouding a bit. "I cannot say that the idea is entirely delightful," he replied. "But... I *feel* real. And everyone treats me as though I am, and so... upon the empirical evidence I must conclude that whatever I have been before, I am real enough now. And I take some comfort in that. After all, there is little use mourning for what has never been, yes? But..."

"But?"

"I worry about Sophia," he confessed. "Is she now as I was, or is she...?" He shook his head abruptly. "But my worries will change little. She is real to me, and I cannot abandon her."

"Of course you can't." Linnea put her hand on his arm. "We'll fix everything--don't worry." But *she* was worried.

Fortune sighed and straightened his shoulders. "Have we time before the food arrives to resume our reading?"

"Sure," Linnea answered. It felt more important than ever to fix her mistake.

They worked for about half an hour until the food came. "Any luck?" Linnea asked Ben as Kurt came back from the door with his fragrant offerings.

"Unfortunately not. I see no mention of my sister at all." He rubbed at his eyes. "This writing is small, and it blurs occasionally. It is a problem I am used to," Ben added, "but it has never caused me quite so much agitation, as there has never been so much at stake before." He sighed and closed the paperback. "I am afraid I'm finding little of use here—instead of acquiring information, I have only made my head ache. And you?" He nodded at the commonplace book.

"No, nothing yet. I'll keep looking," she said, pondering his comments about the writing blurring. "Meanwhile: we need to keep our energy up and... ohhhhh, that smells good."

Without a word, Ben got up and went into the kitchen; in a few minutes she was being presented with a plate containing a wedge of pizza, a helping of chicken korma and a paper napkin folded into the shape of a flower. Kurt followed him, wearing his napkin flower on his head.

Linnea smiled up at Ben a little mistily. "Thanks," she said quietly, and dug in. It was delicious.

"How did you learn to fold the napkins?" Kurt wanted to know.

"Something I used to do to amuse my sister Sophia when she was small," he replied with a shrug and a smile that did not quite reach his eyes.

"So, did I hear you say the words were blurring as you were reading them?" Kurt asked as he shoveled curry and rice into his mouth.

"Indeed," Ben replied when he was between bites. "As I said, it is an affliction I am used to."

"Have you ever considered having your vision checked?"

Ben shrugged. "I have little difficulty riding and hunting; it is only when reading, sometimes. I am well used to it, and need no examination, I am sure."

"Mm." Kurt sounded unconvinced, but let the subject drop.

Linnea was glad to see Ben's expression lighten as they chatted and laughed and fought over the last of the Peshwari naan, which Ben declared his new favorite food. Eventually it was time for Kurt to head out for basketball. He dumped his clean clothes in his room, tucked his ball under his arm, and went out the door, whistling.

Linnea leaned back on the couch cushions and stretched. "Mm, I'm full."

Ben snorted. "A condition to which no lady of my acquaintance would ever admit. But then they were also taught to hold their lips ever pursed, even when speaking, and one can hardly allow for a full bite of food in such a condition." He grinned, his eyes sparkling. "I find I prefer a woman who eats like a human being, and not a hummingbird. As to 'Prunes and Prisms', never has such a foolish practice been invented since time immemorial. I forbade Miss Farthingale to require them of Sophia."

"Prunes and prisms?" she echoed. "What on earth is that?"

"Some ridiculous notion that a woman looks more a lady if her mouth is perpetually disapproving. I'm told they instruct young schoolgirls to hold their lips as tightly as possible and then repeat scripture by the ream." Fortune shook his dusky head. "I haven't the faintest idea who comes up with this foolishness. You ought to have seen Miss Cavanaugh try it around those teeth of hers."

"Poor girl! It sounds like perpetual duckface."

"Duckface?"

"Yeah—something girls do to try to make their faces look better in pictures." She pulled out her phone and flipped through an acquaintance's Facebook profile. "Like this."

Ben did a doubletake. "How odd. And how did her likeness get in there?"

"It's a photograph. See, the phone has a camera—a little like the one used to capture the images on the TV. Here—smile!" He obliged, and she snapped a picture, then showed it to him.

Those dark brows went up. "Is that what I look like to you?"

"Mmhm. The camera sometimes makes people look different," she allowed, "with the lens shape and the lighting. Here, this might be a little better." She turned on the video camera. "What do you think of the twenty-first century, Mr. Fortune?" she asked, holding up the camera.

"I find it fascinating, Miss Santiago," he replied with a good-natured smile. "I am particularly impressed with the company."

"Oh, really? Our little band of blundering misfits?" she said with a laugh.

Ben laughed. "I cannot speak to misfits, for I myself hardly blend with the populace. But I have seen no blundering, only kindness, and the hand of friendship extended."

Linnea smiled warmly and hit the stop button, then scooted next to him so they could watch the footage together.

She knew he had used Kurt's deodorant and soap, but they smelled a lot better on Ben. Her arm was touching his, and she'd never been so aware of him before.

He touched his own image lightly. "Like being reflected in a clear glass, but with sound. Marvelous." Ben smiled up at her. "Now. Demonstrate this duckface for me, if you please."

She began to laugh, which of course meant that she couldn't do it. Every time she almost managed she caught the look of amusement on his face and started laughing again.

He was chuckling too. "It matters not—your own, true smile is far lovelier than any duck's bill. I praise Heaven you have not been subjected to prunes and prisms, as have ruined so many pretty girls in my time."

Linnea pursed her lips and batted her eyelashes.

He gave something between a sigh and a laugh. "No, you must screw up your lips smaller still. As though you are about to be fed something that smells truly vile."

She went more extreme, scrunching up her nose.

He tapped that feature lightly. "No, just your mouth. Just... here." And then his elegant fingers were shaping her mouth. "There," he said softly. "It is still not quite right, but to do more would be a crime against nature." It seemed to Linnea that his fingers lingered before he returned them to his lap, but that might just have been because her lips were tingling. "Now speak a verse."

Her mind sped. What to recite? She said the first thing that came into her head. "Let me not to the marriage of true minds admit impediments," she quoted obediently. Of course, it came out sounding like, "Lit me nit ti the murige iv true munds edmit impidimints," and Ben began to laugh.

"No, I beg you, say it properly. It is a favorite of mine."

She smiled broadly and repeated it correctly.

He rested his chin on his fist, smiling softly as he finished it with her: "If this be error and upon me proved, I never writ, nor no man ever loved." And then the return of that mischievous grin. "No man ever loved Araminta Cavanaugh, I'll swear to that."

She laughed aloud. "Tell me about your first meeting."

He made a face. "I thought you knew all about that."

"I know what it says in the book, but the book also says you were in love with her, so..."

"Oh, I see." He thought for a moment as Linnea settled in. "As I recall, I'd lost a young hound—it got separated from the pack somewhere, and as there was a storm coming on, I didn't like to leave it. So we searched it out, and sure enough, the rain came down as though it had something to prove. The pack ran home to the kennel. I sought closer shelter, and knocked upon the door of the conservatory of my nearest neighbor, whom I had not yet met.

"I could see well enough through the window: there was a large pink mound strewn upon the floor, rather like a pile of strawberry whip. When I knocked, the pink mound resolved itself into a young woman who was kind enough to let me in, which I did appreciate, as there was a river of water pouring down my back from my hat brim.

"She'd been weeping, that was clear enough. I made my introduction, as was proper. There's a type of girl," he added, seemingly apropos of nothing, "who flutters and trembles and goes all faint at the very presence of a man. Araminta Cavanaugh was one of those, as though the sound of my voice would somehow rob her of her innocence or a simple touch of the hand affiance us. Silly cow."

Linnea snorted in amusement.

"Well, after a few awkward moments, her aunt showed up, behaving as though I'd just had my way with the girl, demanding my antecedents, my income, my holdings... I tell you frankly, I became angry, and took my leave before the rain was fairly over. And that was my introduction to Araminta Cavanaugh."

Linnea chuckled. The entrance of Virulea she had been prepared for.

"And now you owe me a story, Linnea Santiago. When did you first begin reading eighteenth century chick-lit novels?" His black eyes were twinkling.

"And where did you pick up *that* vocabulary, I'd like to know!" she said, sitting up mock-indignantly. "Kurt has a lot to answer for."

"You were here when I heard him say it." His eyes lit up. "And then you called him a chauv—I forget the word. What *is* chick-lit, please?"

"Literature for chicks—women."

"And this is a derogatory term? What was it you called him?"

"Chauvinist. Meaning he has a prejudice against women—what we'd call sexism. He doesn't, of course," she added quickly. "He was only teasing me."

"I see." Ben nodded. "All right, a less inflammatory question, then. Mm... Will you tell me about small Linnea Santiago? I confess to some curiosity about your childhood. Is it... too forward to ask?"

"No, not too forward." She gathered her thoughts. "Well, my parents are from Puerto Rico, originally. Dad's a botanist—that's how I got the name Linnea."

Ben's brows went up. "After Carl Linnaeus—a man of my own time. Fascinating. Do go on."

"Mom was a professional ballerina with the Pennsylvania Ballet, but she quit when she got pregnant with me." Linnea gave a little laugh. "Apparently I was a bit of a surprise baby."

"A ballerina?" he repeated, clearly surprised.

Linnea began to laugh. "Sorry, I didn't remember how much things have changed. Okay, so first of all, ballet is considered a high-brow art form now in its own right, like opera. So the Pennsylvania Ballet is a ballet company, like an opera company. And the dancers are no longer considered little better than prostitutes, either," she added, her eyes twinkling with amusement. "It may relieve you to know that my parents were married long before she got pregnant with me." She nudged him with her elbow to show she wasn't upset with him.

"I promise you, I was thinking no such thing," he protested, holding up both hands. But of course he had been; she could see it in his relieved expression.

He was quiet for a little while. "I have been trying to remember more of my childhood, to answer M—Susan's questions in better detail, and I find everything… fuzzy. I suppose it must not have been very remarkable, that I can hardly remember it—only certain events truly stand out." Those dark brown eyes studied her face for a moment as he chewed on his lip. "You have memories, do you not? Favorite activities as a child, or special events?"

"Sure." She regarded him worriedly. Had bringing him out of the novel hurt his memory, somehow?

"Will you share some of them? I revert to my earlier query: tell me of small Linnea, please. Did you like to garden with your father, or dance with your mother, or did you make your own road in all ways?" His gaze was very soft, for some reason.

She grinned. "We didn't really have any space to garden, growing up in Philadelphia, but Dad and I did plant terrariums in our apartment. And yeah, Mom took me to ballet lessons. I only did it through ninth grade, but it made me a really good jumper when I played basketball in high school. But generally, when I was a kid, I played with my little brother Tomás."

"What did you like to do together?" His brow was furrowed, and he rubbed the place between. "I have no recollection of ever playing with Sophia—only of amusing her from time to time."

"We used to play burglar and victim," she told him merrily. "I figured out how to pick the locks on our bedroom doors, and one of us would lie down in the bedroom with the lights off and pretend to be asleep, and the other one had to open the lock silently, so as not to 'wake up' the other one. I used to make scavenger hunts for him, too. I'd give him a note with a clue on it, and he had to follow that clue to the next note, and so on. Oh!" She sat up. "And we used to make forts with the living room furniture!"

He was completely bewildered. "Forts? With—show me," Ben demanded. "Will you?"

She got up, laughing. "We don't have as much furniture here as in my parents' apartment, but..." She pulled the cushions off of the couch. "Go get the chairs from the table, would you?"

He obliged, bringing two at a time.

The two of them arranged the furniture, cushions, throw pillows, and blankets, under Linnea's direction, until they had a creditable fort, one they could both fit under—if they squished together enough. "Come on!" Linnea urged him, laughing.

Ben crawled in, grunting as he avoided clocking his head on one of the chairs, and huddled next to her. "But—what is it *for*?"

"Just for fun! It's like you've made your own little world. The inside of the house becomes the outside, and now the fort is the new inside! Hang on, we can make it even better." She scooted out of the fort, rummaged in the closet, and came back with a string of Christmas lights. "Here, string these up inside," she said, plugging them in, and turned off the living room lights.

Ben looped them over their heads, tucking them behind the edges of the chairs and around the cushions. "Like this?"

"Yep! Now we're camping!"

He looked about, then grinned, settling in. "And now what: stories about the campfire? Or the—the small colored lights?"

"They're Christmas lights—we hang them on Christmas trees. But yeah, we can tell stories. Or watch a movie, or something."

"And which would you like to do?"

"Oh, either. Know any good ghost stories?"

"I—" He frowned again. "I fear I do not. You must, though."

"Oh, yeah, a couple of them."

Linnea settled in and told some of her favorites. "And when she untied the ribbon... *her head fell off!*" she finished one dramatically.

Ben snorted, and then began laughing.

"Hey, these stories used to send Tommy and me to bed with nightmares!" she objected, but she was laughing, too.

"I'm sorry, it just..." He waved his hand, still highly amused. "It's a very comical image, her head just... just... *plop!*" And he was off again.

She laughed along with him, enjoying the sight. He was even more handsome when he smiled than when he was looking dark and brooding, she decided. She loved the enthusiasm he had shown for his new circumstances: it was charming.

He lay back on one of the pillows, multicolored lights reflecting off his face and hair. "I like these forts of yours," he told her, reaching to touch a blue light. "I wish I had known of them in my own youth."

"I imagine some creative children must have put together such things in the nursery," she mused. "Before their nurses caught them, at least."

His brows drew together. "Yes, I'm sure you're right."

She grew concerned again. "Are you sure you're all right?"

"Of course, why should I not be?" Ben gave her a quick smile. "It is only that I... have forgotten my schooldays. Except that I was an excellent student, in a difficult school. But," he said heartily, patting her hand, "we have already determined that my own memories have little to offer in the way of diversion, whereas *you* I find an endless source of interest. And so you grew up... you said in Philadelphia?"

"Yeah."

"Philadelphia—the City of Brotherly Love. I have heard of it—is that not where Mr. Franklin came from?"

"Yep. Good ole nudist, womanizing, weirdo Franklin," she teased.

He joined in her laughter. "I have heard those things, as well. But for you to be from such a place—it makes sense, to my mind."

"Oh?" She lifted her eyebrows and sat up straight. "From the same city as a womanizing nudist?"

It took a moment for Ben to control his mirth, his black eyes merry, hands up in surrender. "No, nothing of the kind! It was ill-put of me, forgive me. I meant that you would be from a place of *Philos*, a city dedicated to kindness and friendship."

"Ohhh." She slanted him an amused glance from under her lashes. "Apology accepted."

"I am relieved to hear it, for it is only the truth. I've yet to hear anything foolish, selfish, or vain come from your lips. You use your mind and are proud to do so, and you encourage others to do the same; you do not judge, but encourage." He lifted a hand as though reaching out, but stopped short, letting it rest on the back of the sofa instead.

She was touched by his sincerity, but found herself shying from it too, so instead she made a joke. "I'll get a big head if I keep listening to you."

"Do you accuse me of flattery, madam?" Ben pretended to be affronted, but his eyes were still twinkling.

"I don't know about *accuse*..."

He grinned suddenly. "More in the nature of stating it baldly, then?"

Her lips twitched. "I just meant that 'accuse' implies I'm not *enjoying* the flattery."

Ben shook his head. "And 'flattery' implies flummery, and I am only speaking truth. As I shall ever do," and then he turned red again.

"What?"

There was a moment of silence, and then, "It was I," he blurted out. "The statue, at the library. I only wanted to see how the everlasting flame worked when there was no flame, and the whole thing just…" Ben looked at her, chewing his lip. "It just fell apart."

Linnea stared at him for a moment, then threw her head back and chortled with laughter.

"You don't seem to understand—I have defaced public property," he explained, brow furrowed at her amusement.

"Oh, you didn't mean to. But you put out the eternal flame!" she hooted.

"Yes, I know," was his guilty reply. "Though in my defense there was no flame to begin with, only a flickering. Still—"

"Ben, the undergrads have knocked that torch off at least three times since I've been going here. It's super loose. Could've happened to anyone."

"Really?" The relief evident in his voice colored his cheeks again. "Oh. That—is good to know." Ben offered her a tentative smile. "Then I shall worry about it no more."

"Don't." She patted his knee. "You haven't put out any flames—just a battery-operated torch."

He relaxed visibly, his dark gaze studying her face with evident pleasure—and then he leaned a little closer and asked, "What's a battery?"

Chapter Six

Linnea slept much better that night, and was in a pretty good mood as she got up to her alarm and took a hot shower Sunday morning. They brought Ben here; there had to be some way to send him home. Yeah, they'd changed the novel, but it wasn't the end of the world. She could do this.

He was examining the toaster with delight when she came out of her room. "It pops up when finished!" Ben told her with some excitement. Before him sat a small mountain of toast on a plate. The toaster obliged with a ding. Ben chortled in delight and began rummaging for more bread.

He'd showered too—that was a luxury he could not stop enthusing about. His damp head was curling a little wildly, his t-shirt was clinging to his biceps and back, his feet were bare. Ben loaded in two more slices of bread and pressed the toaster button, chuckling as the toast-to-be disappeared into the toaster's slots.

Linnea shook her head, amused. "You gonna eat all of that toast?"

He looked at the plate, then at her, rather like a guilty golden retriever. "It's such *fun*," he protested.

She laughed aloud at that. "Yes, it is. And I'll help you eat it. Maybe I should introduce you to Poptarts?"

"Certainly—I shall be delighted to make any acquaintance you like." He smiled down at her. "But first I should like to ask you about attending services. It is Sunday—when do we go?"

"Oh. Uh…" Linnea felt herself blush a little. "I don't… usually go to church? I go with my folks on Christmas and Easter, but that's… about it. Did you—*want* to go to church?"

His brows climbed. "Oh. I—er—we need not, if it is not—" He cleared his throat. "In my time, of course, almost everyone always went, every Sunday. I mind the last time, Miss Cavanaugh would not cease leering at me like a besotted goat. At the collection, I moved my seat to sit directly behind her so she could not do it." His voice drifted off, a small frown appearing. "Yes—I recall that clearly enough."

So did Linnea. Araminta had taken it as a sign that he wished to be closer to her. Linnea watched Ben worriedly. "Well, I don't really have a church here. And—well… I'm Catholic, you know." She knew that anti-Catholic sentiment was widespread in Regency England.

"Oh! I—hadn't realized." Color was climbing up his cheeks. "I shan't bother you with it again, then.

One lapsed Sunday shall surely not damn my soul, Devil though I am. And surely I shall be home by the next."

Linnea's heart sank a little. She couldn't be so sure of that. She fetched some butter and jam from the fridge and sat down to help him eat the mountain of toast.

Ben took the seat opposite and waited his turn at the condiments. "Such sweet jam you have in your time," he said somewhat stickily a short time later. "Indeed all I have eaten here is filled with more flavor than anything in my experience, just as the colors seem brighter, and the people more filled with life." He scratched his rough cheek, wincing as he felt his jaw.

Linnea examined his face. What a very handsome face it was, too. "You're getting a bit of scruff, there," she observed, reaching out to touch his chin with one finger.

Ben rubbed his chin ruefully. "Yes, I know it— Sophia likens me to a 'hairy Esau.' I was hoping to ask Kurt whether he knew of a place where I might be properly shaved but..." He blushed. "As you know, I have no funds."

"Oh, most people do it at home. Come on!"

She led him to her bathroom and opened up the cupboard, handing him a washcloth, a can of generic shaving cream, and a woman's disposable razor. "Bright pink, for manly men." She waved it at him.

He raised a brow at her. "You are making jest of me, but I fail to see the joke," he returned good-naturedly.

104

"People consider bright pink a feminine color," she explained.

"Really? How odd, unless one is Miss Cavanaugh, who regards it as her signature color." He shook his head. "How I do wish I could stop bringing her up, like a meal that has not sat well."

Linnea sputtered with laughter. "Okay, hot water and the washcloth!"

"And I am to do what with them, wet my beard?"

"Yep! Just like your valet's always done before shaving you, I'm sure!" She hopped up on the wide countertop and watched him. "*Did* you have a valet?"

He chuckled. "Of course. Why do you think I am so utterly hamhanded?" He tried to balance the hot washcloth on his face, with little success.

She took over, rubbing it over his chin. "What was his name?"

"Edwards," he managed around her efforts.

"Alright, now you shake the can of shaving cream."

"The can of—oh, this." He obediently shook it up. "And now?"

"We take this cap off... and then you aim the nozzle into your palm and press the button on top."

Looking back, she probably ought to have done that part for him, for once the wondrous foam began to pour from the can, Ben was too enchanted to remember to take his finger off the nozzle, and they ended up with a pile of shaving cream roughly the size of a throw pillow. "Now this is something like!" he exclaimed, very excited.

She tried to stifle her amusement behind her fingers. "Okay, now put it on your face: like Edwards used to do with that little brush."

He scooped up two large handfuls of shaving cream, but this time she was quick enough to stop him. "Here, let's put some of this aside," she said, scraping most of it off of his hand and depositing it on another wash cloth.

"Too much?" he asked, confused.

"Waaaay too much." This time she couldn't hide her expression as she helped him to spread the shaving cream over his chin, contemplating his face. He really was the handsomest man. But it wasn't just his looks that were attractive. His enthusiasm for the modern world, his quick intelligence, his sense of humor...

His lids drooped at the contact, and he made a soft sound of enjoyment as she smoothed the lather over his cheeks and neck, and then used her forefinger to gently wipe it from his lips.

His lips were so soft... She tried to make light of it. "You make that face when Edwards shaved you?" she quipped, but her voice was quiet.

"Generally I lay back in a chair with my eyes closed, so it's entirely possible. This was always my favorite part of my morning routine. Perhaps I shall call you Edwards from now on," he teased.

"As you wish, Sir," she said, dropping her voice to do her best Jeeves impression. "Now open your eyes.

I've got to show you how to do this part." She pulled the cap off of the safety razor. "Here's how you do it!" She held his chin still with the fingertips of one hand, and ran the razor firmly up his cheek.

He frowned. "Why is it shaped like that?"

"So there isn't a lot of bare blade for you to cut yourself on." She rinsed it off and then held it up for him to see. "Two blades, so it cuts closer and is less likely to slice your skin. See?"

He squinted and moved closer to the mirror. "Not as clearly as I would like to," he admitted.

She frowned at him. "Do you often have this problem? Seeing things up close?"

"My sight is... adequate, though I often hear my friends describe details which I cannot perceive. Why?"

"Maybe you need reading glasses."

"Half-moons? My dear girl, I am but two-and thirty! What sort of quiz would I appear, even in so accepting a society as yours?"

She laughed softly at this evidence of vanity. "They wouldn't be half-moons: we could get you a really sexy pair," she teased, wiggling in her seat on the counter.

He noticed that, all right, dark gaze dropping to half-mast again. "What is this 'sexy'? I have heard the word before, but its meaning is not clear."

"Mmm... attractive to the opposite sex," she said diplomatically. "Veeeery attractive. Also known as *hot*." She grinned.

He chuckled, though low, so as not to interrupt her work as she scraped away his stubble. "And these glasses you describe would be such a thing?"

"Absolutely! Here, you try." She handed him the razor.

It took him a moment or two to figure out how to hold the razor and how to flatten his neck, but his first swipe was successful, though he was squinting terribly as he did it. "Yes?"

"Yes." She took the razor back. "But I'll do the rest of it—until we get you a pair of sexy glasses. Maybe they'll be pink," she added innocently.

"And I can wear mutton stew in my hair," he replied, dimples deepening in each cheek.

"And say prisms and prunes all day long! Then you *will* look a quiz!"

"Clearly I am destined never to be sexy," he said mournfully. She gave an involuntary snort at that.

When they had finished, he wiped his face with the wet towel, smoothing his hand over his chin. "Well done, Edwards. I shall put an extra silver in your week's packet." Ben reached to help her hop down from the counter.

She did so nimbly—then picked up a small handful of shaving cream and flung it at him. "SNOWBALL FIGHT!"

He ducked—barely—and then scooped up a handful of the cream and lobbed it at her head, daringly.

She shrieked and dove—a little too late. It covered her shoulder. She scooped up the rest of the cream and flung it directly onto his chest.

He made a sound of protest and picked up the can, firing a stream at her shirt.

She squawked indignantly, grabbed a damp loofah from the shower, and threw it at him, smacking him in the eye.

His hands went up. "I yield—I yield!" There was shaving cream in his hair and all over his shirt. He bent to rinse the foam from his forelock in the sink, then stood and shook like a puppy to get rid of the excess water, spattering Linnea liberally. "I shall have to change my shirt," he observed mildly.

"Well, go do that, and then we'll go buy you some glasses."

Linnea had to change, as well. When she came back out to the living room, Ben was comfortably ensconced on the sofa, in a sprawled-out attitude that almost exactly echoed the way Kurt sat. He'd put on a blue t-shirt with an exploding TARDIS on it, and he smiled as she came into the room.

"Hey," Linnea smiled back. "Ready to go get some glasses?"

His expression was an interesting mix of trust and worry. "And I shall not look a fool?"

"Not at all," she assured him firmly.

Ben gave a decisive sigh and a nod. "I am, as always, in your capable hands, Linnea."

She grabbed her purse and keys. "Then let's go!" she said brightly.

He hung back, just a bit. "I will find a way to repay you, my friend. Not truly, for I owe you far more than I can possibly—but your money, that I shall find a way to replace."

"Oh, reading glasses cost less than ten bucks a pop. Don't worry about it."

He followed her out the door. "What is a bucksapop?"

His tone made her giggle. "Ten dollars—ten bucks—apiece."

Brows drawn together, he questioned her closely about the American monetary system on the way to the store. "So it is all based on units of ten. A simpler system than I am used to, for which I am grateful. But you say a penny is nigh worthless now?"

"Yep, pretty much. It's the same in Britain, which has also gone to a decimal system. The results of inflation."

He shook his curly head. "In my day a penny would have bought you a good loaf of bread."

"Well, no more. But at least they sell us our bread already sliced, so that's an improvement," she said with a grin.

"Indeed it is," he replied, rubbing his hands together. "Excellently prepared for toasting."

She laughed at that. "And sandwiches. I'll make you some for dinner."

110

"Linnea," he said after a moment, "you need not wait on me. I know you and Kurt do not have servants and must do for yourselves. I wish to help, not add to your burdens any more than I already do."

"Oh, I'll show you how to load the dishwasher and help with the laundry," she said calmly. "We'll get you pulling your share," she added, giving him another smile.

"I shall do more, to ease your burden. You are a lady, by any standard, and should not have to sully yourself with menial tasks."

"And what menial tasks do you imagine I perform?" she asked, curious.

"Cleaning, cooking, laundry—I do not imagine it, do I?" He looked both confused and embarrassed now. "Forgive me—perhaps I should not have said anything."

She shook her head, amused. "All three of those tasks are much easier these days, with the technology we have, but you're free to help if you want. And don't worry about mentioning the servant thing. Only the super, super rich have servants these days."

"Really? I hadn't—well, I hadn't really thought about it, until I arrived here," he admitted. "But I wish you will teach me all that you do, so that I may do my fair share while I am here."

"Okay, no problem. But there really isn't much."

A moment or two went by. "Still, it seems to me that having help to run a household of any size would still be beneficial. Why are there servants no longer?

Except for the super, super rich," Ben added conscientiously.

"It's the economy," Linnea explained. "So, in your time, goods were pretty expensive, but service was really cheap. That's why impoverished gentry could afford hardly any new clothes, but still had a serving maid and a man-of-all-work. Now, it's the opposite: goods are pretty cheap, but service is really expensive. That's why I've enough plenty of food in my pantry, but I have to wash my own dishes." She smiled over at him as she parked the car.

He hopped out and ran around to open her door, bowing elegantly. "Then I shall be your man-of-all-work, while I am here, my lady Linnea, and you shall want for nothing," he said teasingly, black eyes twinkling. "Nary a dish shall you wash—once you have taught me how," he added with a laugh.

She chuckled too, touched by his gallantry. "You shan't wash a dish either: the dishwasher shall. But I'll make you Swiffer the kitchen if you keep that up. C'mon."

"Swiffer," he muttered to himself as he held the door of the store open for her.

She took him to the eyeglasses section of the store, by the pharmacy. "Now, we've got to figure out what prescription you need, first."

She helped him through the process of figuring out which strength of lenses he needed, by looking at a card with various sized writing on it through different pairs of glasses. When they figured out his prescription, she pointed to the rack of glasses. "Here are the ones in the strength you need. Here, what about this?"

He tried on pair after pair, looking at her helplessly. "You choose—I have no idea what looks well."

She tried a couple of styles on him and finally settled on a pair of silver wire-rims. "Here. What do you think?" She pointed at the mirror.

"And they do not make me look a quiz?"

"Not at all! Look." She pulled a more feminine pair of wire-rims off the rack and put them on. "See?" She struck a pose.

His smile grew warm. "How can I tell if you do not make a duckface?"

She complied, trying not to laugh.

Ben's answering laugh was full-bodied. "Sold then, if they are not too dear."

"Not at all. A steal at seven bucks."

"But they are for close viewing only, yes? The world looks quite odd otherwise," he observed, squinting through them.

"Yeah, you can take them off whenever you're not reading. That's what the case is for. Or you could just put them on top of your head." She smiled up at him.

He took her by the shoulders. "Hold still, please." Glasses in place, Ben studied her face, her hair, a smile quirking the corner of his lips. Goodness, he was even more handsome up close...!

"Examining my pores?" she asked innocently. "I promise, I washed my face."

"No, just learning details I missed before. You have a freckle by your eye, just here," he very nearly touched her. "I had not seen it before."

She caught her breath, but in a moment, she said quietly, "But can you see the little scar where my brother accidentally hit me in the face with a stick when I was seven?"

He moved closer; she could feel his breath softly on her skin. "Just barely. But there is no beauty where there is not imperfection. And it is only a very little scar."

She looked up into his dark eyes, still beautiful behind his glasses, barely breathing.

"Amazing," he said, and it took her a second to realize he meant the glasses. "I'd no idea what I was missing. As, indeed, I feel about most of my life, now I think about it." He stepped back, and the moment ended.

"How do you mean?" she asked, still feeling a little breathless.

Ben was quiet for a moment, gathering his thoughts. "Last night, as I lay waiting for sleep, it occurred to me that at home, in my world, I am a secondary character in someone else's story. And I have felt so, all my life. Even my birth—" he broke off there. "But now I feel... different."

"How do you feel now?" she asked, curious.

"Promise not to laugh."

"I promise."

He fiddled with the glasses. "As though I am living my own story, and not someone else's."

"I don't think there's anything funny about that," she assured him. "I think it's awesome."

"A hyperbolic use of that word, I assume, since you are unlikely to be actually awed by my small revelation." He smiled at her. "Cool."

Then she really did laugh.

A voice spoke up behind them. "Hello, Mr. Fortune!"

They turned to see a woman with dark hair and lively eyes. Ben smiled. "Dr. Bialecki! How very nice to see you again."

Susan's adviser gave him a friendly nod. "Likewise. You really had me going the other day, you know."

"Had you... going?" Ben's expression grew troubled.

"Yes—you really had me believing you had the name Ben Fortune but had never heard of the book! Susan set me straight." She laughed good-naturedly. "I had an uncle who used to do that—make up ridiculous stories just to see if he could get people to believe them."

"Oh—I—er—yes, ha ha," was his unconvincing return, his cheeks growing red. "We met on an onsite webline." Ben cleared his throat. "Allow me to introduce my friend Miss Santiago. Linnea, this is Dr. Bialecki, Susan's adviser, who was kind enough to help me in the library."

"Pleasure," Dr. Bialecki said, shaking Linnea's hand. "Are you also a student at Sunhill?"

"Yeah—a PhD student in history," Linnea answered.

"Aha. What in particular are you studying?"

"The John Key archive at the library."

"Oh!" Dr. Bialecki's smile widened. "How fascinating! Are you going to do any study abroad work to see his other manuscripts? Especially since you have a friend in Rosebury-on-Wye," she added, sending a little teasing wink Ben's direction. He seemed completely nonplussed by this, and looked at Linnea questioningly.

Linnea shook her head, amused. "I don't have the Bens to afford that kind of thing."

"Oh, but you do! You have a Ben right here!" Dr. Bialecki joked delightedly, pointing at him.

Ben was mystified by this. "I do beg your pardon: 'Bens'?"

"Short for Benjamins," Linnea clarified. "A nickname for hundred-dollar bills."

Suddenly Ben looked relieved, as though here was something he could field. "Ah—no, my name is not Benjamin, if you will forgive me." He smiled pleasantly at Dr. Bialecki. "My given name is Benoni Jabez, though I do not use it, and prefer to go by Ben. Others have made a similar error," he added kindly.

Dr. Bialecki's eyes widened. "D—did you say *Benoni Jabez*?"

He nodded. "I'm told it is an odd name—even comical," he added, glancing at Linnea. "Thus I go by Ben alone."

"Yes," the professor answered, apparently at random. "Yes, I suppose so."

"Oh, hey—we've got to get to that thing," Linnea said, tapping Ben's arm. "Sorry to run—so nice to meet you!"

"You too," Dr. Bialecki answered distractedly as they hurried away toward the checkout counter.

"To what *thing* do you refer?" Ben hissed under his breath as Linnea paid for his glasses.

"I just wanted an excuse to go," she answered in an undertone. "I was afraid she was going to start asking more questions, and we don't have a good enough cover story worked out yet."

"Oh." Ben glanced back at the professor, who was still watching them, a strange expression on her face.

Chapter Seven

After lunch, Linnea drove to campus to scan more materials from the archive, and picked up Ben's clothes at the drycleaner. Back at the apartment again, Ben wanted to finish reading Burnworth's novel, now that he had his new glasses. The new clarity of the pages seemed to be distracting him from the content, however. "Astounding!" he would say every few moments, or "Amazing!" He looked up at Linnea. "School would have been so much simpler had I these then."

"I bet. You must've had terrible headaches."

"I—yes, I suppose I must." He bent his head back to the novel, finally closing the back cover, stroking it with gentle fingers. "There is nothing here of Sophia. I can find not a single mention of her anywhere."

"Well, there's only one mention of her in the original version, and you're the one who brings her up. Don't worry, though; we'll keep looking for a spell to send you back." There was a pause, and she frowned. "Why do you think you don't remember anything?" she asked at last.

Those dark eyes sought hers. "I have wondered that myself, and I cannot much say I like my conclusion."

"Which is?"

"That there is nothing for me *to* remember."

"What do you mean?" Linnea asked, confused and a bit alarmed.

He put his glasses on the book and got up to pace around a bit, as though the room had grown too small for him. "This book of yours, this *Fortune's Folly*—it bears my name, but it is not my story. From all that you have said, all you have shown me, the entire book is from Araminta's point of view. Is that correct?"

"Yeah?"

He nodded. "Then despite the title, despite my—my *existence* here in your world, in my own I am merely a secondary character. Whatever I know of myself came from an author who had no need to—to flesh me out. I *feel* whole, and yet—I do not think I am. Or was," he corrected himself, running his hands distractedly through his hair. "I think, when off the page in your book, I simply... faded into a colorless half-life until needed again. Here, it is... different."

Linnea's eyes widened. "That's... kinda super creepy," she said at last.

He shrugged. "I said I did not much like the idea. But for all that, I do not think I am wrong."

Linnea opened her mouth to answer, but was interrupted when a yawning Kurt emerged from his bedroom, shirtless and in loose green scrub pants, scratching his belly. "Mornin', or whatever the hell time it is," he mumbled, and headed for the fridge to pour himself some orange juice. Fortune gave him a Look, but as Linnea said nothing about her roommate's language or state of undress, neither did he.

"Look at you, all conscious and everything," Linnea said, unwilling to start the conversation again in his presence.

Kurt rubbed his hand over his face. "Sez you," he returned. "What time is it, actually? Day off, no alarm."

She glanced at the time on her phone. "Almost five."

"Okay. What's up for dinner, any ideas?"

"Frozen pizza?" Linnea suggested.

Kurt made a rude noise with his lips. "Okay, I guess we already did the takeout thing this week. You want some help with that while the pizzas are in the oven?" He nodded toward Key's notebook.

Ben picked up the notebook and peered at the crabbed script. "Things are far less blurry than they were, but this is rather like trying to decipher the dance of a drunken cockroach."

Linnea laughed. "A cucaracha doing a cha-cha! We can take a break," she assured Kurt.

Kurt turned on the oven. "These'll be done in twenty and then there's some pickup down at the court on 4th, if you guys want to come play. Or watch." He went into his room to get changed, and Ben turned to Linnea for explanation.

"Basketball. It's a game."

"From which I deduce a ball and a basket. Is this something you enjoy?"

"Yeah, I used to play in high school."

He smiled. "I look forward to watching you play, then. Are there rules I should know?"

She spent some time running down the basics; by the time Kurt took the pizzas out of the oven, Ben claimed to have a decent grasp on the subject.

They ate, worked on the notebook a little more, and then Linnea changed into something more appropriate for basketball, and they headed out.

Ben was fascinated, watching Kurt handle the ball as they walked. He passed it around one hand and then the other, spun it on one finger, and generally showed off. Fortune was suitably impressed.

When they arrived, someone by the name of Bolt (perhaps due to the lightning bolt depicted in his closely-shaven hair) was picking teams. "Aw, no," he protested at seeing the threesome. "You can't put Kurt and Nae-Nae on the same team."

"Hell we can't, and we are," cried someone else, whose hat said his name was Lakers. A third young person whose identity wasn't immediately clear gestured to Fortune. "How about him, he playin'?"

"No, thank you," Ben himself answered. "I don't know much of the game and would only slow you down. I'd prefer to watch, if I may." It seemed to be 'aiight' with everyone, so he found himself a seat on a bench at the side of the court and settled in to watch.

He soon learned why Kurt and "Nae-Nae" weren't to be allowed on one team. Watching Linnea initially made him wince—the other players gave her no quarter for being female; though as he knew Linnea, she wouldn't want them to. And she gave as good as she got, being swift of foot and generally fearless. Ben wasn't sure of the exact moment when concern for her wellbeing gave way to blood-lust, but he found himself on his feet cheering when Kurt planted his feet hard, tossed the ball high, and Linnea placed one foot on his thigh, another on his shoulder, and *launched* herself into the air to grasp the ball between her hands and slam it hard though the hoop.

To judge from the disgusted expressions on the faces of the opposing team, this maneuver was frowned upon. "Oh, *here* we go," muttered Bolt, as a laughing Linnea dropped from the hoop. "We playing with the effing Globetrotters, man."

Kurt was waving his hands. "Come on, come on, we got it out of our system. We'll even take a penalty for it."

Linnea took the opportunity to make her way over to Ben, panting a little. He offered her the water bottle Kurt had suggested he bring along. "You are a formidable opponent, Linnea—or should I call you 'Nae-Nae'?" Ben smiled up at her.

She shrugged, smiling back. "Been a stressful week, you know? But that *was* just showing off."

122

Somebody blew a whistle, and she jogged back onto the court for the penalty throw.

After that Ben just watched her: the way she moved, lithe and strong, not at all like the mincing, fainting women of his own day. She and Kurt read each other well; Ben knew enough of team sports to recognize why their friends didn't want them on the same team, acrobatics notwithstanding. They were good players separately, but together they dominated the court. Linnea was a rough player, not afraid to slam into her opponents, male and female alike, in driving the ball down the court. Ben spent a moment trying to imagine the women of his day playing such a game, but all he could picture was mewling mounds of muslin and watered silk all over the court, the ball forgotten as each player claimed a turned ankle and waited for a man to come carry her to a chaise and praise her for having fallen on her arse so gracefully. He began to laugh quietly.

Linnea came over again, grinning. "What's so funny, Baloney?" she asked.

"Baloney?"

"Baloney Benoni," she teased, dropping onto the bench next to him and taking big gulps of water.

His lips quirked as he opened the bottle of water he'd brought for himself and took a drink. "I thought of something amusing, that's all. You look warm."

"Very. In fact—" she stood up and, to his great shock, tore off her trousers, to reveal considerably shorter ones beneath.

123

Ben nearly broke his neck turning away from her as quickly as he could. After a moment the feeling returned to his scalp, and he thought he'd best play the whole thing off as a joke. "You might have warned a fellow."

She chuckled. "Sorry."

What a very odd world he'd landed in, he thought, returning his gaze to her. Very well, he could adapt. "Just as you like, Saucebox. Perhaps this will help cool you as well," and he poured some of his water down her back.

She gave a yelp and began laughing. A few others nearby, who had witnessed his prank, began laughing, too. Linnea jogged back onto the court.

He hid a smile. What a world indeed—and what a woman of it, he thought. So filled with life and color, making him long for things he hadn't the words to describe, so used as he was to half-tones and half-light. A half-life.

The group on the basketball court played on, Ben only partially paying attention, lost in his own thoughts. But he did notice, a few minutes later, when one of Linnea's opponents came in toward her, moving fast. Linnea was in an optimal position and held her ground, leaning into the coming crash. The two collided pretty hard, and Ben was on his feet even as the referee, a young woman in a yellow shirt by the name of Akeelah, blew a short blast on her whistle. "Foul," she called.

He had some idea what that meant but didn't care; he just wanted to know that Linnea hadn't been hurt. She didn't seem to be: the players lined up, and Linnea sank the ball easily in the basket.

"All right, all right," panted Bolt after about another half an hour. "I promised the kids we could find some Nemo before bedtime." He wiped his forehead with the hem of his shirt.

"I'm out too," chimed in Lakers, whose name had turned out to be Jay. "Promised Pauline I'd take her to that new jazz place."

"Okay then, next week?" asked Akeelah, and almost everyone nodded. "You too, Lin. We don't see enough of you. Bring your boyfriend too—he's easy on the eyes. 'Night, everyone."

Kurt and Linnea pulled their extra layers back on: the evening chill was becoming more pronounced. "Are you warm enough?" Ben asked his companions as they walked home.

"I'm fine," Kurt replied. "Hot shower and I'll be all set up."

"Yeah, I'm good," Linnea smiled up at him, tendrils of her hair plastered to her brow.

He began to reach to brush them back, and then suddenly remembered where they were, who he was, and more importantly, who he wasn't. So he scratched his nose instead.

Soon they were home again. "I'm heading out with the guys," Kurt announced, "but I'll be back around midnight," to which Ben replied he would certainly take the couch; and after retrieving pillows and blankets, he went to forage in the refrigerator as Kurt's bathroom door closed.

"I'm going to get a shower and go to bed. You need anything else?" Linnea asked.

"Hm? No, I shall find a way to entertain myself. I can always look over your notes on Key's writing," Ben replied with a short laugh.

"Well, have fun!" Linnea smiled.

Linnea woke to the scent of bacon and eggs. She staggered out to the living area, still in her pajamas and bleary-eyed.

Ben was humming to himself as he fried a rasher of bacon. "One egg or two?" he asked her, adding a couple of crisp strips to the pile of pork on the paper-towel-covered plate next to the stove.

"Uh... two," she said blankly. "Um... How did you learn to use the stove?"

"There is an entire television channel devoted to the culinary arts, did you know? And the instructions are quite intuitive," he indicated the knobs. "And I have watched you, as well." Deftly he tore holes in the center of some soft slices of bread and tipped them into the frying pan, breaking an egg into the middle of each. "Fried egg in toast," he informed her with a grin. "Hard or soft?"

"...Hard?" Linnea sat down in one of the kitchen chairs, in awe. "You are... *amazing*, you know that?"

126

Those brows flew high. "I? Not in the least, I am only become used to puzzling out my surroundings undetected." He served her up her breakfast, including several pieces of bacon.

"That probably doesn't usually include deciphering electronic kitchen appliances," she pointed out, but ate her breakfast with enthusiasm. "This is *good*!"

"'Tis a staple over a campfire in England or in France," he said with a shrug. "Easy enough to translate to a stove, even one with knobs." This last was said with a grin as he wiped down the countertop. "Had I potatoes, now, that would have been a *feast*."

"Well, write up a list of the ingredients you need, and I'll get them!" Linnea promised.

He finished tidying up. "Miss Ray on the television said to put the leftovers away in the 'fridge'," he began, "but I was unclear as to what 'plastic wrap' was."

"Oh! That's this stuff." Linnea fetched it out of a bottom cupboard and showed him how to use it. He pulled out a sheet of his own and immediately became entangled in it.

"Ingenious," was his comment as he tried to free his thumbs. "No, do not help me—I *shall* prevail."

She watched him, chuckling. "Okay, I'm scheduled to work in the archives today, so I'm going to do some more searching through Key's papers. Do you want to come with and hang out in the library, or stay here?"

He shrugged, managing to smooth out the plastic sheet, more or less. "I have the images of the notebook here to search, but otherwise feel I would add little to your studies at the archive, and," a dimple made a brief appearance, "would be far too tempted to distract you. I have your number by the phone should I need to call— or I can call Susan, or take a walk, or do any number of other things. Truly, Linnea, I shall be fine."

"Okay. Here—I'll give you my house key in case you want to take a walk. Just be sure you're back to let me in by six."

"I promise." Ben gave her a mock salute. "Enjoy your shore leave, Captain Picard."

Linnea stared at him for a moment, then went off in a peal of laughter. "Make it so, Number One!" she crowed.

He grinned the whole time she was heading out the door.

Linnea skimmed through a great deal of the box that day. She catalogued very little, and knew that Dr. Helman would be on her back come the end of the week. But she was searching for something specific, and Dr. Helman would just have to wait.

As a matter of fact, he didn't. Linnea was poring over some papers when her adviser was suddenly reading over her shoulder, breathing stertorously. She nearly jumped out of her skin. "Miss Santiago," he greeted her startled face, thick mustache quivering, brown eyes large and somewhat liquid, like a golden retriever's.

"Geez," she panted, trying not to clutch her chest. "Hello, Dr. Helman."

"How are you today?" he asked with perfunctory politeness, eyes still on the page before her.

Oh, just recovering from a heart attack. "Fine—how are you?" *And what the hell are* you *doing here?*

"I came to see how you were getting on," he answered her unspoken question with every appearance of eagerness. "I'm hearing good things about your research—though of course I know how hard you're working. Quite a feat, though, exciting the interest of Nadine Bialecki. I wouldn't have thought Key to be up her alley."

"I—uh—wha?" Linnea managed intelligently.

"Dr. Bialecki, one of the lit professors. She mentioned you'd described some of your work, seemed quite interested." He chuckled avuncularly. "As I say, arousing interest in the history of philosophy from one who spends the greater part of her passion in the realms of imagination: quite a feat. You whetted her curiosity—we had rather a lively discussion over coffee earlier. Anything of particular interest this week?"

"Uh—no, not yet. I—don't remember which part of Key's work I told her about. What did you two discuss?"

"Mm," he pursed his lips, "oh, a wide range of subjects. She seemed most intrigued by what I could tell her of the essay you catalogued recently on the subjective reality of fictional characters."

Shit. "Oh. Right."

"Anything else in that line?" he asked would-be casually, though she could see the banked fires of Jankyism begin to glow in his eyes, tongue all but lolling out.

"Nope, not a thing! Back to laundry lists," she answered quickly.

He didn't bother to hide his disappointment. "Pity. Well—do keep me posted. Excellent work," he added, and sauntered from the archive, his hands deep in his hairy tweed pockets.

The encounter rattled Linnea a little, and she found herself dialing the house phone, just to check on Ben. His hello was a bit breathless. "What have you been doing?" she asked cautiously.

"Something called Zumba, and watching a few other shows," was his equally cautious response.

"Okay," she chuckled. "Don't break anything. I'm including yourself in that."

He laughed, and they finished their conversation. Linnea sat in thought for a moment, then called Susan.

Chapter Eight

Susan agreed that she and her girlfriend Rose would meet them at Linnea and Kurt's for dinner, by which time Linnea hoped to have found something useful in Key's papers.

She didn't.

She headed home by six, finding the door open as promised. The sound of the dishwasher clued her in that he had taken her warning of dinner guests seriously; he'd even tidied up the living room, bless his heart, and had put linens out on the table, and candles and her only set of actual candlesticks.

The man himself was nowhere to be seen, though there was a light coming from under Kurt's bathroom door, and there was the faint sound of humming. "I'm home!" she called.

The bathroom door opened to reveal a damp, curly, half-shaven Ben, wearing his glasses. "Welcome home!" he greeted her, careful not to give her *too* much of an eyeful, though from the evidence of his broad shoulders, he hadn't put a shirt on yet.

Linnea bit her lips with an involuntary smile, then gave a wolf whistle, just to tease him.

He brightened. "I know what that means! You are sexually harassing me! Though I find I do not mind it much, considering the source."

She crowed. "You're damn right I'm harassing you! By the way, Martha Stewart, thank you for doing up the dining room. It looks great."

He toweled off the rest of his face and came out into the hall, a second towel secured around his waist. "Since you have thus set the tone for the evening, I shall adopt the dress of one of the more sought-after young men on *Guides of Our Family Days*, a most enlightening program. I could hardly look away."

Linnea bit her lips again, her eyebrows moving into a new and exotic formation. "You—you were watching soap operas?" she asked, her voice sounding strangled.

"There was no singing that I recall. Quite a lot of kissing, and a really rather inordinate amount of implied fornication. Everyone seemed quite skilled at it, and no one was ashamed of themselves in the least." He left the question implied.

"Um..." She swallowed hard and tried to speak normally. "Premarital sex is... uh... far more accepted today, especially what with effective contraception and all. So you... liked *Family Days*?"

"Effective...? Oh, I see. It does explain why Gingham City wasn't awash in infants. Although there were several times when a—er—sheath would have

132

been unlikely to have been obtained. What methods are commonly practiced, then, that frolicking spontaneously in a forest would have seemed like a sensible course of action?" He was barely holding in his own laughter, those black eyes twinkling.

Linnea started chuckling. "Okay, good, you *didn't* take it seriously."

"Surely you do not take me for such a blockhead! These people were making love every ten minutes on the average, in between two kidnappings, a secret identical twin, and an interrupted nuptial, and those were only the plot points I understood! All was enacted with such *urgency*, however." He did laugh, finally. "We did have overblown dramatics in my time as well, Miss Santiago, though with fewer... bath towels."

"Oh, really?" she said, lifting one eyebrow and looking pointedly at the one he was currently wearing.

Color crept into his cheeks, but he firmed his jaw. "From what I witnessed today, my current attire is considerably less revealing than some, which I am given to understand causes no one concern. Do I not measure up to your whistling? I believe my alternate choice of outfit was a pair of jeans left mostly unbuttoned, and a shirt but only without the sleeves. Shall I go change? I *do* so wish to fit in with your culture." He batted his eyelids at her, lashes impossibly long and black.

She burst out laughing. "Please *don't* dress like a soap star for dinner tonight."

"Just as well—I should need the constant assistance of a breeze to stand in. I shall require your guidance in the matter of my dress, then."

She went into Kurt's room and helped him pick out something, trying not to think about his state of undress. She wasn't entirely successful.

At her behest he ended up in jeans, fully fastened, and a button-down shirt which he did actually button down. "I have a confession to make, Linnea— 'twas not I who was Martha Stewart, but Mrs. Lopez from 2067A."

"Oh, you met María?" Linnea pulled out her collection of takeout menus.

"I heard some shouting," he began the story, "a lady clearly in distress. Hercules had slipped his lead, which I am given to understand is not unusual for him, and was heading for the park across the intersection, heedless of traffic. Suffice it to say that he and I have had a very stern discussion, master to hound."

Linnea raised her brows. "You managed to stop him?"

Ben grinned. "I have raised dogs since I was a pup myself: of course I stopped him. Mrs. Lopez brought me lunch, we watched her shows, and she very kindly explained them all to me, in between suggesting I go somewhere called Hollywood so that I too may raise an eyebrow enigmatically at the camera while standing bare-chested in a convenient breeze." He flushed again, though he was clearly amused.

Linnea went off in a peal of laughter. "California, here we come!"

Ben tried to practice his enigmatic eyebrow on her but kept chuckling instead. Finally he gave up, grinning. "Clearly I am not cut out for Gingham City. What is the plan for dinner?"

"We'll get some delivery when everybody gets here," she answered lightly. Mrs. Lopez wasn't wrong, though: Ben Fortune was... well, *devilishly* attractive, just to look at. When he was like this—when she could see his personality, his humor, his teasing nature (hinted at in the books, but only just)—when he was at his ease, Ben Fortune was downright *lethal*. Enchanted though she was, Linnea was prevented from further banter by the ringing of the doorbell.

Peering from behind Susan was a young blonde woman, who looked Ben over pretty thoroughly and said, in a soft southern accent, "You really weren't kidding. If that's *not* Ben Fortune, I'm Araminta Cavanaugh."

"I hope, for all our sakes, you are not," he returned with a smile, "and so I must be Ben Fortune after all. You must be Miss Rose."

"Got it in one," she said, grinning as they came in. She wore a sundress and cowboy boots, her short blonde hair in an undercut.

"Kurt should be home soon. What do you guys want to eat?" Linnea asked when all the introductions were finished. "Pizza? Chinese? Thai?" She gestured to the takeout menus on the coffee table.

Ben was busy examining the label on the bottle of wine the women had brought. "'Platypus with Shoes'? Is this an Australian vintage, then?"

Rose laughed. "No, just a small label with a big sense of humor."

"I haven't had Thai in a while," Susan suggested. Kurt came gangling in as they were poring over the menu, and soon they had their order in and Linnea was serving the wine.

Ben tasted his. "Really rather lovely," he pronounced. "Crisp. Not a hint of vinegar, which is often how wine was judged in my day."

"Have you guys seen this? #FFFail is trending on Tweeter," Susan said, pulling the app up on her phone.

Ben's brows went up. "I can make a guess at the 'FF' part. *Fortune's Folly*, yes? What's a Tweeter?"

"A website—has Linnea explained the internet to you yet?"

"Yes, to some degree, as did Mrs. Lopez. I know it is an internationally interconnected web of information, powered by electricity and supported by satellites in orbit around the earth. What sort of website is this Tweeter, social media?"

"Yes!" Susan and Rose both looked impressed. "Yes, exactly. It's a way to post just short messages."

"Wait," Rose said. "Who is Mrs. Lopez—does she know about you?"

"She is a neighbor—I helped her with her dog," was the edited version Ben gave.

"But how did you explain that you needed to know what the internet was?" Linnea asked, suddenly worried.

He grinned, pure mischief. "I told her I had to stay in character, and asked her to help me by explaining everyday things to me."

"In character—like an actor?" Susan laughed. "What character did you say you were playing?"

"Why—Ben Fortune, in the special lecture Linnea is giving, a few months hence." His grin broadened. "It turns out Mrs. Lopez is a *fan* of the novel."

Rose laughed. "And if she wasn't *before* meeting you, I bet she is now!" she sang out. He blushed but didn't demur.

Linnea had taken Susan's phone and was scrolling through the tag. "'I wanted to read FF tonight—then remembered I can't anymore. #ThanksObama,'" she read aloud.

"Your former president, yes?" Ben commented. "What has he to do with this?"

"Nothing. That's the point. Oh this—oh, never mind; I'm not reading that one out loud."

Kurt grabbed the phone, looked at it, and whistled. "Wow, people are *ticked*."

"And hysterical," Rose nodded. "You should see the fansites."

"Fansites?" Ben's ears pricked up. "I should like to see one, since I am supposed to have met Susan over one."

137

Susan took her phone back and pulled one up. "You should read the fanfiction," she said, grinning wickedly.

"Ooh, yeah," Kurt added. "Make sure to look for the ones rated 'Mature'. You wouldn't want to read the ones for kids," he added, all innocence.

"Stop that," Linnea said, snatching the phone back. "Do you want to scar him for life?"

The doorbell rang, and they soon laid out all the food. "I have something a little... worrying to report," Linnea told them over tom yum goong and khao pad. "You know how your adviser Dr. Bialecki met Ben? Well, we ran into her at the store yesterday, and she acted a little strange, and since then she's been to see *my* adviser, and was grilling him on my studies and John Key's essay on the reality of fictional characters."

"Come on," replied Kurt through a mouthful of food. "She can't possibly suspect, unless she's nuts." He looked around at the others. "Can she? You think that's a logical leap: this guy has a name like in a book, and he looks like the guy in the book, so he must *be* the guy from the book, especially since the guy in the book is now missing..." He subsided. "Wait, maybe this *isn't* good."

"Yeah. That's what I'm worried about."

"In what way did she act strangely?" Susan wanted to know.

Ben shrugged. "Not knowing the woman well, I can't speak for her usual manner; but she seemed quite taken aback at my name, and stared at me rather uncomfortably afterward. Until we had left the shop, in fact. It was a bit off-putting, but I merely thought I was misinterpreting things." He rubbed his fingers through his hair. "I do so easily, here."

"No, it was definitely weird," Linnea backed him up. "Like, why would she be so shocked that you've got a weird name? Lots of people do. I knew someone once named Nimrod Morshitz. Benoni Jabez Fortune is basically John Smith in comparison."

"Well, if anything, that's likely to send Nadine *off* our tracks," Susan pointed out. "The novel just calls him 'Ben Fortune,' and anybody who didn't know him personally would figure it was Benjamin, not Benoni." She shrugged. "Maybe she was just curious about her new acquaintances. She's really nice, in my experience."

Ben touched Linnea's hand lightly. "Then perhaps we should not worry unduly over trifles such as these. As Kurt so rightly pointed out, it isn't likely to be the first conclusion one would draw."

"True." Linnea smiled and took a bite of her dinner. "I guess I'm just a little paranoid, especially with how upset and frightened everybody is about the novel changing."

Ben put down his fork, chopsticks having proved to be beyond his skill. "I confess I too am worried about the changes as I hear them reported. It is strange indeed to consider oneself as a character in a novel. My only concern is how I might return, and set things right."

Rose shook her head. "I just can hardly believe you really were a fictional character."

His dark eyes gleamed; he gave her a small smile. "Yes, and I am grateful for the past tense. I have spent some little time wondering what I shall be now, when I do go back."

"Huh." Rose pondered for a moment. "...What was it like?"

"By comparison to here, now?" Ben twirled the stem of his wine glass. "It was gray, or at least half-colored. I've little recollection of laughter, or joy, except in the company of my sister Sophia. But even there, it is all just a morass of... moments." He shrugged. "I don't know how better to explain it."

Susan looked intrigued. "Because you were a secondary character," she said slowly.

He nodded. "That is my own conclusion," he said softly. "I was there, God save me, to give dimension to Araminta Cavanaugh's story. And probably to be some sort of cautionary example."

Susan nodded. "Because she must wait for a man to speak, a woman is often trapped by her own desires when that man cannot or will not admit his passions, even when they are obvious to all," she said, sounding like she was quoting something. She looked around at their faces. "At least, that's the scholarly conclusion."

"What's that from?" Kurt wanted to know.

"One of the best-known academic publications on the novel," she shrugged.

Ben sipped his wine again. "Did it truly occur to *no one* that the reason I didn't pursue her was because she was an unbearable chit with a unique, and not particularly appealing, personal fragrance?"

Linnea nearly snarfed her wine, and Rose went off in a peal of laughter. "Really? I would *love* to hear the story from your point of view."

"RIGHT?" Susan exclaimed. "My point *exactly*. As I shall discuss exhaustively in my dissertation."

"Really?" asked Kurt. "You gonna out him in your dissertation? Or try to convince your adviser that we did a magic spell?"

"Of course not!" Susan looked affronted. "I'm just going to say I think that the stories of secondary characters are very intriguing."

Ben looked gratified. "Really?"

"Yeah, it's the entire point of my dissertation. Based on quite a number of late eighteenth and early nineteenth century novels. It's obvious from a lot of them—like *Fortune's Folly* or *Emma*—that changing to a secondary character's point of view would change the entire story." She paused, frowning. "That's a question," she said slowly.

"What is?" Ben wanted to know.

"If you're a secondary character, and if that means that all the events in your life that weren't specifically mentioned in the book kind of didn't happen to you... Then how come you know your name is Benoni instead of Benjamin? *That* isn't in the book!"

He blinked, clearly confused. "Because it… is my name?"

"But… Okay, let's do a quiz. On the day that you met Araminta, when you took shelter from the storm in her aunt's conservatory: what did you do after you went home that evening?"

He thought for long moments, brows drawn together. "I cannot precisely recall. I probably read for a while—I am an avid reader—or tended to the business of my estate, as all gentlemen of my time do."

"But you don't remember? Did you tell anyone about the meeting? About her crazy aunt or her smelly hair?"

"N—no, I would hardly do so. One never knows when the servants might be listening. And no, I don't remember that specific evening." He sighed, fidgeted. "I recall very few specific evenings. As I said—a collection of moments, and all apparently shaped by Araminta Cava—" Dark eyes went wide. "Oh! But—*she* does not know my full name! I see what you mean. And yet—and yet it *is* my name, I know it is."

"Exactly." Susan sat back in her chair. "So why?"

They were all silent, contemplating this. "It shouldn't be possible," Rose said slowly. "Your backstory ought to be limited to what's in the novel. And yet…"

"And yet," Ben finished, "here I sit, and I know what I know."

"And I know that you guys are a bunch of downers!" Kurt interrupted them. "We should be playing dinner party games, like they did in Ben's time! You know—'Hunt the Slipper'." He wiggled his eyebrows suggestively.

Susan gave him a Look. "Number one, how the hell do you know about Hunt the Slipper?"

"Hey—I read," Kurt said defensively.

"—And number two," Susan continued in a slightly louder voice, "it's really not as sexy as you're making it sound."

"You mean it's not a euphemism?" Kurt looked seriously disappointed.

"Oo, I've got a *wicked* idea!" Rose suggested, pulling out her phone. "They've managed to reconstruct the original novel," she announced, "using quotes from various sources and people's memories. Maybe Ben would like to read it?" Her eyes twinkled.

"Oh, Lord, I don't think I'm drunk enough to spend time in Araminta Cavanaugh's wee little mind; but if it will amuse you." Ben spread his arms wide. "Give me the guillotine and I shall see how well it fits."

They laughed and Susan poured more wine into his glass. "Well then, let's get you buzzed first," she allowed. She waved her phone at Ben, who pulled his new reading glasses from his pocket and perched them on his nose. Susan paused. "Wh—uh, those look— nice."

Rose cleared her throat. "The 'get-out-of-jail-free' card applies only to Tom Hattleson's version."

Susan made a face at her girlfriend and handed Ben the phone, who looked quizzically at them.

"I told you they were sexy," Linnea murmured into her glass.

"I have missed something," Ben concluded, but when no explanation was forthcoming, he turned his attention to the book. "Oh, that ball. I recall it well."

The shift of expressions across Ben's handsome face as he read this account was as good as a play. He read it through, only having to pause once to collect himself. "Well. Would you like a scene-by-scene breakdown, or shall I just take myself off quietly somewhere to be sick?"

They were all chuckling. "Just tell us what's so awful about it!" Kurt grinned.

Ben ran his hand through his curly hair. "Lord, where to begin... Well, it is obvious why the company drew back at Araminta's approach. The truth is that whenever Virulea Cavanaugh and her niece arrived anywhere, there was a general exodus from the ballroom. But it had more to do with the elder Miss Cavanaugh's sharp tongue and even sharper manner, when prey in the form of an unattached gentleman was sighted. As to Araminta's toilette—I have already told Linnea the worst of it, and since we've all just eaten I shan't repeat it—but what she refers to as 'pale pink' was in reality a rather startling shade of rose pompadour, and if your imaginations can stretch to an entire ensemble in such a color... And my wager would be that poor Louisa Ferrars, who looked very nice in a

144

lovely blossom pink with broderie of white peonies, was merely trying to avoid a scene."

"What kind of scene?" Linnea asked avidly.

"Oh, Araminta giving her loudest sympathies on how pink was such a *trying* color for most ladies, who would do well not to attempt it, though fortunately she was gifted with the ability to wear it well. I have speculated now and again whether there was something off with her eyesight, that she should choose such colors to wear, but perhaps the fault was the author's, and not Araminta's own." He paused and took a healthy draught of his wine. "That is easily the strangest thing I have ever said."

They laughed. "What else, what else?" Linnea asked, bouncing.

"Lord." He scanned the device. "Well, she wasn't wrong—I was avoiding her. Would have run screaming into the street if I'd had to. The strong feeling that she refers to me suffering under was that I was going to disgrace myself. At length I took refuge in the card room."

"What about Colonel Braveit?"

Ben chuckled. "Bit of a scamp, old Braveit. I expect he found it all amusing. Dashington was a friend of his, though—he wouldn't have allowed Araminta to bring poor Dash to a declaration on the dance floor."

"And yet she does, later." Susan nodded sagely. "She marries Dashington." Her expression of certainty slipped. "At least—she did originally."

"So I found, poor chap. She shan't get much pleasure from that alliance, I'll wager." Ben went red. "Forgive me, ladies. But poor old Dash would have been the last I'd have expected in that particular hangman's noose. He... wasn't much of a ladies' man; generally kept himself out of the fray. But I suppose... based on my own experience with Miss Cavanaugh..." He huffed out a breath. "Have you ever met someone who simply would not hear what you wished to say?"

"Yeah?"

"So she was, and skilled at it indeed. Worse, she could take something you said from pure politeness and twist it into what it was never intended to be." Ben tapped the phone lightly. "Here, where she mentions my cousin the Viscount—I'm still not sure how she did it, but I was never so grateful to be interrupted in my life."

"Wait!" Linnea sat straight up in her chair, startled by a prick of jealousy. "Are you saying you actually *were* going to offer for her??"

"*No!*" was the emphatic reply. "I was *trying* to do the opposite, to tell her politely that I would make no such offer, but she kept twisting everything I said—I can't explain it." He toyed morosely with his wine glass. "I said she must have mistook my feelings, she said true love was never a mistake—I agreed in principle, and suddenly she threw herself upon my bosom and was caterwauling some nonsense about her damned aunt's disapproval—" Linnea relaxed, grinning. Ben made a face at her. "I'm glad you're amused. For myself, it was like seeing my life flash before my eyes—such as it was.

146

I admit I was a trifle foxed at the time, and had no idea why her aunt should disapprove of me, so I asked, which she took as some kind of declaration of undying devotion... Anyway, Charles came in and peeled her off like the limpet she was."

Rose was laughing. "Bottle's almost empty—last calls for refills! What shall we drink to?"

"Convenient viscounts?" was Ben's suggestion.

"I like it!" Kurt cheered. "Convenient viscounts!" They all raised their glasses.

Everybody drank, laughing, and then Ben clinked the rim of his glass to Linnea's. "And to brilliant researchers who give life to their studies—literally." He drained the last dregs of his wine.

Chapter Nine

"Well, we probably should get going," Susan said at last. "Thanks for having us!"

"Yeah, thanks for coming!" Linnea said, getting up to give her a hug. "It was great meeting you, Rose."

"Likewise. Next time, you guys come to our place, and I'll cook. Can I pick up your Faceplace from Susan?"

"Of course!" Linnea saw them to the door.

Kurt loaded the dishwasher and then grabbed his sports bag. "You guys wanna come to pickup?"

"Oh, I'm so full of Thai, I don't think I can," Linnea answered, stretching.

Ben just smiled and shook his head, to which Kurt replied, "Which reminds me—I've got a date with Melanie after, so the bed's all yours tonight." He wiggled his brows and waved as he left.

Linnea plopped down on the couch. "Well, that was fun."

"It was," Ben agreed, stretching out his long legs. "Tell me about 'fanfiction', please."

She laughed. "It's when people take their favorite stories and rewrite them, or add new characters, or put themselves in the story, or write sequels..."

"Ah, yes. People did so in my time, as well, though I expect they found less circulation. And why would I be scarred by these?"

"Because in some of them, various characters from the novel have erotic adventures," Linnea grinned, wiggling her eyebrows suggestively.

He thought about that. "You mean that I and Araminta—?"

"Yes. Or you and a new female character. Or you and Lord Dashington—that seems to be a popular pairing." Ben began to laugh, shaking his head in disbelief. She grinned. "Or you and your cousin the viscount. Or you and—"

"Oh, come, Linnea. You do not truly expect me to believe anyone would take such interest in me as to put pen to paper and create such outrageous fictions?"

"Oh, they totally do. Some of them actually have you coming forward in time and meeting your fans. Well, falling in love with one of them, usually. Or you and Araminta running a coffee house. Or going to a modern high school together."

He laughed all the harder. "Now I *know* you're bamming me. Who would read such tosh as that?"

"Alright, smartass." She pulled out her phone and began typing. "How about this?

Ben gave her a look, probably in response to her name-calling, and then adjusted his glasses and peered over her shoulder. "Are you telling me that's one of these... fanfictions?"

"Yes indeedy!" She giggled manically and, leaning back so that he could no longer see the screen, began reading dramatically. *"'No, Saffron,' Fortune growled as he took her in his arms. 'I do not love Araminta. I'm in love with you.'"*

The real Ben's brows climbed nearly off his forehead. "Saffron??"

"Saffron bit her lip, white teeth sinking into plush, ripe flesh. Warmth suffused her body: her cheeks flushed, a delicate mantle of color that only made her lovelier. Lower, her body responded to his, heat gathering and pooling in twin points behind her bodice, and lower still, in her secret glen of desi—"

"STOP," Ben demanded, his own cheeks mantling rather frantically.

Linnea was giggling again. "Oh, come on! Don't you want to hear the part where the viscount joins them for a threesome?"

Fortune's mouth worked for a moment. "N—no, I certainly do *not*," he stammered at last. "Oh, Lord." He cleared his throat, pushing his glasses back to the top of his head. "I thought my supposed romance with Araminta Cavanaugh was the passion that set a thousand hearts beating—why take her from the story and create such... illicit nonsense?"

"Well, there are still plenty of Fortuminta fics," she said, scrolling on her phone some more. "But fans are so attracted to you as a character... they just want to have you to themselves. Besides, not even all the Mary-Sues—the stories like that one, with a new female character—are explicit. And some of them are actually really well written."

His eyes were very dark indeed. "And is that the sort of story you read?"

"Um... sometimes."

"And other times?"

"Oh, sometimes I read Fortuminta. Or other fandoms."

"Such a ridiculous portmanteau word, Fortuminta…" He shook his head. "And which is your favorite?" He'd relaxed, crossing his long legs at the ankle. "Barring the other fandoms, of which I have no knowledge."

"Oh, I like them both. Though I don't think I can appreciate Fortuminta anymore like I used to."

"I'm sorry," was his soft reply. "I've stolen your pleasure."

"No, no." She smiled. "Getting to know you has been the far greater pleasure of the two."

He answered her smile with one of his own. "Supposing we were in one of your well-written fanfictions now." He spread his arms along the back of the sofa. "What would be happening?"

"Oh, we'd probably be exposing our deepest, darkest secrets, followed by making out." She wiggled her eyebrows at him.

"Making—out?"

She made a loud kissing noise.

"Oh, Lord. Even the well-written ones?" Ben sighed. "Let us ignore that part. But as for the other..." He was thoughtful for a long time. "I don't think I have any secrets from you, but as I am fictional, I suppose I could make one up?"

"Actually, there was something I was curious about. You don't have to tell me about it if you don't want to," she added quickly, "but you've mentioned your father a couple of times—in reference to your name, for one."

"I will tell you anything you like."

"Why was your relationship with your father so... fraught?"

Ben was matter-of-fact. "Because he hated me, I suppose."

Her eyes widened. "For heaven's sake, *why*?"

"He believed that I murdered both my mother and my older brother, the *proper* heir. It was from him I gained the nickname 'Devil' Fortune, actually, when he took me to school. 'Just rid me of this devil,' he said to the headmaster. Or so I recall." Ben shrugged.

Linnea reached out and took his hand. "Why on earth did he think you had murdered your mother and brother?" she asked, bewildered. Ben could never have done that sort of thing—well, very few children could! And where was all this backstory coming from, anyway? It wasn't in the novel...

"My mother died in her confinement. My twin brother—the heir, he would have been—was stillborn. The doctor tried to rid her of the afterbirth, so she should

152

not bleed to death—but instead he delivered me unexpectedly, and Mother died anyway. My brother was christened Benaiah at his graveside: 'delivered of God.'

"And Benoni?" she asked quietly.

"Son of my sorrow," was the soft reply.

She scooted closer and wrapped her arms around him in a hug. "I'm so sorry," she said quietly. "That was cruel of him."

He went very still, and then slid his arms around her, holding her lightly. "I suppose Father must have been rather a cruel man. I don't recall much of him, to be honest. Still, in the end he trusted me with Sophia, so he must not have hated me so very much." He smiled down at her. "This is very nice. Is it your turn to tell me a dark secret?"

"Well, I can if you want, but I'd like to hear about Sophia," she answered, not moving from her spot.

"She is—she was—sixteen, impertinent as you please with her respected guardian brother, and has my coloring." He tugged gently on one of Linnea's curls. "Darker than these pretty locks—more like coal than chocolate."

She smiled. "So your father remarried?"

His brows drew together. "Yes, and Sophia was born when I was twelve. I didn't attend the wedding—only met Sophy when she was six already, and I was about to head up to Oxford. There was a month between terms, and Father let me stay at home."

Linnea gave him an extra hug and was silent.

Ben leaned his chin on her head. "It's all right, you know."

"It was wrong," she murmured. "Wrong and cruel."

"But I had Sophia, and will have again. And now I have you. And Kurt and Susan and Rose," he added conscientiously.

She smiled, but it faltered after a moment. When she found the spell, he would go back into the novel, and she would never see him again.

His mouth drooped; evidently he was thinking of the same thing. "I have another deep, dark secret, Linnea."

"Yeah?" she asked softly.

"I will miss you."

She gulped, tears coming unbidden to her eyes. "I'll miss you too," she said softly.

He thumbed them away. "No, don't. Don't cry, Linnea." He gave her a sweet smile. "It's just a book."

That made it worse. She shook her head and buried her face in his chest.

Ben just held her, stroking her hair. "I have another question," he murmured after a while.

"Yeah?" she answered, her voice muffled by his shirt.

He moved his hand, stroking her jaw with his thumb until she looked up at him, and he smiled again, his gaze very gentle. "To what did Rose refer by a 'get-out-of-jail-free card'?"

Linnea gave a little chuckle, sitting up a bit more. "Some couples have a little list of famous people they're allowed to... sleep with, if they ever have the chance. Apparently the actor Tom Hattleson, in the role of Ben Fortune, is on Susan's list."

His brows went up. "I was under the impression that Susan and Rose are in a—Sapphic relationship."

Linnea grinned at his terminology. "They are, but Susan's bisexual—she likes men, too."

He chuckled. "How very egalitarian of her. And you are smiling again, which is my infinite preference."

Her smile turned a little forced at this reminder of the subject they'd been discussing, and she sat up, breaking the hug.

He frowned slightly at her withdrawal. "What have I said?"

"I just don't like the thought of you leaving," she said lugubriously. "I know you have to, but—I wish you didn't." She heaved a sigh. "We need a lighter topic. Would you like to watch a movie?"

"I am at your service, of course."

"Not at my service," she said, giving him a more genuine smile. "What do YOU want to do?"

Ben gave a helpless laugh, lifting his shoulders. "You say that as though I am the one who knows what my choices are. You could tell me that the latest entertainment is to stick one's head in a beehive, and I would simply cry 'Capital!' and follow you along like a very large and slightly stupid puppy."

She laughed with him. "Okay. A movie is like TV. It's a play you watch in your home."

"And there is going to be one of my story with this fellow Hattleson as me and he is exceedingly sexy."

"Damn straight." Linnea pulled up a promo photo on her phone. "That's Tom Hattleson. Look at that hair!"

Ben studied the actor's picture critically. "He looks nothing like me, though he does appear a man of some bearing. And who is the beauty with the primrose hair, some secret love of his?"

Linnea grinned broadly, and was silent.

He looked up at her, then did a wide-eyed double take. "*Never* tell me that's Araminta!" She began to giggle wickedly. He looked at it again. "But—no, it is a joke, you cannot mean..." Ben adjusted his glasses and looked a third time. "But this woman is quite lovely! Her figure is most respectable, and her teeth aren't—" He used his fingers to make rabbit teeth again, and waved the phone at her. "Had she looked like *this*, there would have been scores of men willing to overlook the pomade, let alone that she's an utter lackwit."

Linnea took the phone back, laughing. "Well, that movie's not out yet anyway. Here, come look at my collection." She got up and led him to her bedroom, realizing suddenly that it would be the first time he had seen it. Luckily, she didn't have any dirty underwear lying about.

He hesitated at the door. "Is it—?" But he made up his mind and followed her in.

She gestured to the large bookshelf that held her DVD collection, as well as her textbooks.

Ben tilted his head to read the titles of the movies. "You are a romantic, madam."

She laughed. "Guilty as charged. You up for romance, or something else?"

"Whatever gives you most pleasure, my dear Linnea."

"Well, then how about suspense?" She plucked Alfred Hitchcock's *Rebecca* from the shelf.

It took Linnea a long time to get to sleep that night, but it wasn't from the thought of Du Maurier's mad housekeeper. She kept thinking about Ben—the look on his face as he had talked about his family, the way he had stroked her hair when she hugged him, the warmth of his eyes as he touched her chin. And she made a realization: she didn't want him to go.

Like, *really* didn't want him to go.

In just a short time he had become a friend, and to say goodbye to him now... She shut her eyes with pain at the thought.

There was a possibility, of course, that he *couldn't* go home—that there was no spell to send him back, or that they would never find it. It felt selfish, but... she hoped she wouldn't find that spell.

She woke to lovely, breakfasty smells, and padded out to the kitchen to find Ben in a running outfit:

157

skin-tight, thigh-length shorts, his new sneakers, a workout shirt that *had* to be two sizes too small, and a hoodie half-zipped.

His black curls were damp and sticking to his forehead, and he was serving up a couple of breakfast sandwiches. "Morning," he chirped, handing her a plate.

"Did you... go jogging?" she asked, voice a little choked as she tried not to react to his outfit.

He gave her a sunny nod. "Mrs. Lopez suggested it as an alternative to my accustomed daily ride. She helped me with the apparel—her nephew's, I believe."

Linnea bit back a smile. Clearly María Lopez had a wicked sense of humor, to put him in that too-tight outfit. "You're just full of surprises, aren't you?"

"Am I now?" He looked gratified. "I rather like surprising you. To wit," and he nodded toward the breakfast he'd just served up.

"Is that from Leo's?" she asked, recognizing the wrappers from a local restaurant.

"Yes—it was recommended to me," he replied anxiously. "Is it all right?"

"Oh, yeah. They've got good breakfast food." She took a seat. "But—how did you, um, pay for it?"

He took the seat next to her. "Oh! Mrs. Lopez has asked me to take Hercules to the dog park sometimes since it interferes with her soaps. She paid me today for helping with him yesterday, and there was some left over after I repaid Kurt. And a two-for-one breakfast special at Leo's."

Linnea chuckled. "Good for you, finding a job already! My brother tried for a year before he landed anything." She twinkled up at him as she bit into her breakfast burrito.

"It's only taking Hercules to the dog park. Though she said she had some friends who might have odd jobs for me, here and there, while we are in rehearsal for your interactive class."

"For my—? Oh." Linnea laughed. "Right. My big lecture on Ben Fortune. Well, thank you very much for breakfast! It's very sweet of you."

Eyes twinkling, Ben finished the sandwich, wiping his fingers on a napkin. "Well—I must launder these clothes and return them to Mrs. Lopez. Are you at the archive today?"

"No, today I'd usually be working on my own research at home. I'll keep going through my scans."

"So you will be home this morning?" Ben's dark eyes were filled with pleasure when she nodded. His dimples deepened, though he said nothing more, heading toward Kurt's room to clean up and change his clothes.

To Linnea's astonishment, the Ben that returned with his arms full of laundry was dressed in full Regency regalia, from windswept hair to cravat to boots.

Her eyes widened: she hadn't seen him in those clothes since the first night he had appeared in their living room. Her brain immediately went on the fritz.

159

"Uh—what are you doing?" She couldn't manage anything more articulate.

He paused, winged brows rising. "I am laundering these clothes, as I said I would do." Those black eyes studied her. "Are you quite well, Linnea?"

"No, I mean—in your Regency clothes?" She cleared her throat.

"Oh." He looked somewhat abashed. "Mrs. Lopez has asked if I would enact a scene or two as 'Ben Fortune' at an…" His brow furrowed with the effort of trying to get the phraseology correct. "Assisted living facility? She has been so kind, I felt it would be ungallant to refuse."

Linnea turned a laugh into a cough. She needed to cultivate the acquaintance of María Lopez. The woman had a devious mind.

Ben laundered the too-tight jogging outfit, and a little while later Linnea bid him a smiling goodbye, wishing she didn't have to keep researching so she could watch a bunch of sweet older ladies thrill to meeting Ben Fortune in the flesh.

The research yielded nothing, and Linnea was feeling rather down by the time Ben returned that afternoon. He, too, seemed distracted when he came in, tugging at his cravat, though his smile for her was ready as always.

"How did it go?" she asked, summoning up an answering smile.

"Hm? Oh, well enough. Everyone seemed most pleased." His eyes gleamed with a hint of mischief. "I

160

imitated your 'fanfiction' and pretended that each woman there was my own true love instead of Araminta. They seemed to enjoy it. And Mrs. Lopez was well-satisfied, which was my first object. And you?" He relieved himself of cravat and coat and sat next to her in waistcoat and sleeves, the neck of his shirt gaping a bit.

"Man, I wish I could have been there. Nothing new to report on the home front, I'm afraid."

He nodded, still looking somewhat introspective, studying the toes of his boots. "I recall riding upon my estate," he began suddenly, apropos of nothing, "and to that ill-fated picnic when Araminta— oh, you know the one I mean. And the boots show wear. It must follow that I can actually ride, would you not say so?"

"Uh, yes?" Where was this coming from?

His brows were knitted tightly together now. "It has come to my attention that there are things I can do, that I know how to do, because I have *done* them—in the course of the novel. And that there are other things that I *feel* I know how to do, but only because they are a part of my character as the author intended, not because I have ever actually experienced them." Ben turned to look at her. "For example, I know the rules for chess. I suspect I'm rather good at playing the game. But I cannot recall ever having seen a chessboard."

Linnea blinked at him. "Well that's… weird."

That elicited a laugh, and a general lightening of his expression. "Of a piece with my entire existence, then. Good to know." He got up after a moment.

"Well—I am due to take Hercules to the dog park shortly, so I must change. It would hardly be suitable for me to take him dressed this way." Ben chuckled again. "I should prefer to 'blend in', as Mrs. Lopez calls it; and perhaps the person living in their car across the street will cease their vigilant examination of me each time I go out." He headed for Kurt's room.

"Their—wait, what?"

He paused upon the threshold, his head turned slightly. "The person who lives in the car across the street? They seem to find me an object of interest—well, all of us in this... apartment. I expect it has to do with not having a home of their own, poor wretch. Mrs. Lopez tells me that people often take refuge in their vehicles when they have nowhere else to go. Have you not observed them?"

"Uh, no." She stood up and peeked out the window. "How long have they been there?"

He shrugged. "I first noticed them after we came home from acquiring my glasses. How long they may have been there before that I cannot say. Excuse me, please—I will be late if I do not make haste." The bedroom door closed.

A chill ran up Linnea's spine. She could see the car he was referring to. It was a white station wagon, and sure enough, there was a shape in the driver's seat. Was the person genuinely just homeless—or was someone watching them?

She stood and debated for a moment. She could call the police—but it was probably a misunderstanding.

She didn't have any proof that the person was actually bothering them. Maybe they really were just homeless, in which case she didn't want to call the cops on them. There was also the option of confronting them... but what if they were dangerous? And she had no proof they were actually stalking anyone...

The choice was taken from her hands when the vehicle's running lights came on, and it drove away. Linnea watched it go, frowning.

Chapter Ten

Susan dropped in that evening, reaching the apartment soon after Kurt got home. "Just wanted to come by and see how everything was going," she said, giving Linnea a hug.

"Situation normal, all messed up," Linnea answered as cheerfully as she could. "Ben entertained some ladies at a retirement home by visiting them in the character of fictional Ben Fortune, Regency clothes and all."

Susan's eyes widened. "Pictures or it didn't happen," she rapped out.

Ben's eyes twinkled. "I assure you, it did. There are… pictures, I believe, though I do not have them. Mrs. Lopez seemed quite busy with her phone."

"I have GOT to spend more time with María Lopez," Linnea muttered.

"She is a most congenial lady," Ben agreed obliviously. "And you, Susan? How have you been since last we met?"

"Fine—getting lots of practice teaching literature. At least I can put it on my CV. Nadine's canceled a couple of classes yesterday and today. Comes in for the night classes, though."

"That's weird. Can't be sick—what reason did she give for taking off?" Linnea wanted to know.

"Family issues. Though it would have to be with her parents—Nadine isn't married, and no kids." Susan shrugged. "I didn't want to pry. Nothing new on the research front?"

Linnea shook her head silently. Ben touched her hand unexpectedly, his expression gentle. "You'll find it," he said with quiet confidence. "Of that I have no doubt, Linnea. My life could be in no better hands."

She gave him a small smile. "Thanks."

Ben found himself at loose ends for the next few days: Linnea was expected to put in time at the archives, and was searching for a solution to his dilemma while there. He had no wish to divert her attention, but apart from walking Hercules and another visit to the nursing home, there was little enough for him to do.

Therefore he accepted Kurt's unexpected invitation to 'grab a couple of brews' one afternoon with alacrity.

"Full disclosure—I've got something I want you to do," Kurt said as they drove along.

"Of course, if it is within my means," was Ben's ready reply.

Kurt nodded. "You know I'm a medical student, right?"

"A noble pursuit, healing one's fellow man," Ben agreed.

"Noble, huh?" Kurt's grin was a bit abashed. "I guess. Point is, there's a free program at the hospital for undocumented people to come in and get vaccinated. It's open this afternoon."

Ben mulled this over. "Undocumented—meaning I have no papers, yes? True enough. As to vaccination..." He shook his head. "I believe I have had the Jennerian inoculation in theory, though whether it will prove actually effective in this world I cannot guess. Is it likely I shall become exposed to smallpox?"

His companion gave a snort. "Not at all—we've virtually eradicated smallpox. But we can protect you against a lot of other things. It won't take long."

Ben nodded. "If you believe it is best, then it is what must be done," he replied simply.

As it turned out, Kurt had not exaggerated—Ben endured the injection of several vaccines with mysterious acronyms, all of which served to protect him from illnesses that were considered common hazards in his world. The injection was far less painful than the inoculation process in his own time, and Kurt assured him it would not make him ill. Afterward, they went to a place called a 'bowling alley,' where Ben discovered that bowling had evolved quite drastically from what he was used to: or at least ought to have been used to, as he could not recall ever having truly played. Thus it gave him far greater pleasure in that this time, he actually got to experience it.

"Strike!" cried Kurt gleefully as his ball decimated the formation of pins. "That's another round!" He raised his hand to wave at the barkeep, and soon a young woman approached their lane with a pair of foaming glasses.

This would mark Ben's third of the afternoon, and the effects were interesting indeed: a slight buzzing at the base of the skull and a general feeling of wellbeing. This, then, was what it was to be intoxicated, he concluded. Yet another thing which he might be supposed to have experience of, but of which his creator clearly had no idea.

"You okay?" Kurt wanted to know, peering at him, and Ben realized his attention had wandered.

"I am," he assured his friend. "New experiences, merely."

Kurt laughed. "Old Belinda never went in for beer and bowling, huh?"

"I suspect not," Ben returned, amused, and went to bowl his frame as best he could. Kurt, meanwhile, had spread himself out over the plastic seating, as was his wont, and was watching Ben with curious intent when he returned to his own chair. "Is something amiss?" Ben asked, looking over his person and then back at the bowling lane.

"Nah. I was just thinking." Kurt took a pull at his lager.

"Of what?"

"You, mostly. Your situation, and how weird all this must be for you, and..." He shrugged. "You're not at all what I would have expected."

"No?" Ben was curious. "In what way?"

Another shrug. "Any of 'em. For starters, you look more like today's idea of what a Regency gentleman would look like than the real thing. Tall, strong features, jacked body—you've even got a tan. Too working class. You should be pasty and soft to show how indolent you are."

Ben chuckled. "You are thinking of a fop," he informed Kurt. "I am more of a Corinthian: interested in matters of sport. Riding, hunting, driving, shooting, boxing..."

"Boxing?" Kurt seemed surprised.

"Indeed. Many an afternoon have I whiled away in Jackson's boxing saloon." He paused, wondering about the truth of that statement, then shook his head.

"Huh." Kurt gave this some thought. "Well, I guess that explains your looks, but there's other stuff, too."

"Such as?"

Kurt finished his beer. "You don't seem to care that I'm not white, for one thing."

"Oh. I suppose that's because I don't, really." Ben shrugged. "In my time—or I should say, in my world—the measure of a gentleman was how he treated those who might socially be thought beneath him. Not that I think you beneath me," he added quickly. "I believe in the equality of mankind: what the French

168

Revolution championed before it turned into the Terror. There are many where I am from who might disdain to befriend a man of color merely for his skin, but I should hope I would never be one such."

Kurt digested that. "Yeah, you just pull it off with less badly-concealed condescension than I think a lot of your contemporaries would." He grinned.

Ben smiled back. "I am not sure how much credit I can take for it: I believe Miss Burnworth wrote me to be 'a very parfit gentil Knight'."

Kurt laughed. "Okay, equality of mankind I get. But what about womankind? You seem to take Lin in stride, too."

That was wholly untrue, and Ben took care to let him know it. "I assure you I do not! Linnea is easily the most extraordinary woman of my acquaintance. Her poise, her intellect, her very great heart: all these must set her apart from the vain and insipid young women I have known, including she-who-shall-remain-nameless. She is entirely outside of my experience, and I promise you I value her friendship all the more for it."

Kurt was holding up his hands, protesting. "No, no, I get it! I didn't mean that you take her for granted, I just meant..." He paused. "We haven't achieved equality between women and men by a long shot yet, but it's still got to be worlds different than it was in your time, right?"

"Ah." Ben nodded. "I take your meaning. And yet how could I not value a woman of independent spirit? Indeed, if not for such women I would not exist, either literally or literarily." He gave Kurt a grin.

His friend laughed. "Still, I'd've thought you'd find her unfeminine, by the standards you're used to."

Ben thought about Linnea's lovely face, her warm skin, the dark waves that fell so gracefully over her shoulders, her strong but slender figure... "Unfeminine? Hardly," he said, and found his voice seemed to grown husky.

His friend was watching him. "Huh," was all Kurt said, but Ben felt unaccountably exposed for some reason, and was relieved to put an end to that particular conversation as they went back to their game.

Over dinner that night Linnea got an earful of the wonders of modern medicines. "Can you conceive it?" Ben asked her, more than once. "I cannot now contract measles, nor fetid lung, nor the whooping cough. I have already had the mumps, but I am beyond the reach of lockjaw, and typhus, and something called hepatitis. What miracles medicine has wrought since my own time!"

Linnea chuckled but agreed, amused and touched by his almost childlike enthusiasm for the modern world. But vaccinations were a pretty amazing invention, she had to admit.

A few evenings later he regaled her with the information that he'd been hired as an 'odd-job man' around the neighborhood, on María Lopez's recommendation. "She has very kindly provided me with a character to all of her friends," he told Linnea and an amused Kurt with enthusiasm. "Many of these ladies have small gardens, and I am to help tend to them. One," he went on, frowning slightly, "asked me to clean her pool, but Mrs. Lopez said I should not accept, and in truth I would not know how, so I declined. Though the sum she named seemed quite extravagant for a day's hard work."

Kurt seemed to be trying not to choke on his dinner. "I bet," he managed weakly after a moment. "Sounds like Mrs. Lopez is looking out for you all right." Linnea mentally made plans to bake María Lopez cookies.

She peeked from the curtains throughout the next day, watching Ben move from house to house, mowing lawns and weeding gardens. He came in for a quick lunch and went right back out again, apparently quite happy with his menial labor. It *would* make a change for a Regency gentleman, Linnea reflected, but Ben had been concerned for some time now about his contribution to the household funds and seemed to regard this as an opportunity to repay his inadvertent hosts. Besides, the great thing about physical labor was that you could see the results of your work.

The next time she looked out, she realized Ben wasn't the only one interested in his work: three of her "friendly neighbors" were being friendly indeed, surrounding him in conversation as he took a break from his mowing. It seemed muscular, hard-working Ben was providing a show for all the stay-at-home moms in the neighborhood. They appeared to be jockeying to get closer to a smiling Ben. Linnea's eyes narrowed. The sheer volume of lash-fluttering could probably power a couple of turbines, and if they tossed their hair one more time they were going to blow away all Ben's carefully-raked grass clippings. He, she noted with some wry amusement, was carefully not looking at the bikini one of the women was wearing, with mixed success.

Linnea watched for a minute, expecting him at any moment to say goodbye and start the mower again, but to her growing annoyance, he didn't. She suddenly brought herself up short. He had been working hard; he deserved a break.

It's not the break you're upset about. Linnea tried to shake off the thought. She couldn't be jealous, she told herself. There was nothing to be jealous about. She had no *right* to be jealous.

Linnea went back to what she was doing, and at long last heard the mower start up again. Even then she had difficulty concentrating, and at last gave up and made a pitcher of lemonade.

When she exited the house with two glasses, Ben was across the street, down at the end of the block. She was opening her mouth to shout a greeting over the sound of the mower when Ben turned off the machine and simply shrugged his sweat-stained t-shirt over his head, using it to wipe his face and neck. When he lifted his face from the shirt and caught sight of her he froze, like a deer in headlights.

Linnea realized she had stopped in the middle of the street and was staring at him. Thankfully, she hadn't dropped the lemonade.

Ben was trying to untangle the soggy lump of jersey when she approached him. "I do beg your pardon, Linnea," he managed, cheeks bright. "I thought myself unobserved."

The curtain of the house they stood in front of swung slightly in a nonexistent breeze. Unobserved, sure: fat chance of that. "That's okay," she answered as brightly as she could. "Here, I brought you some lemonade."

"Oh—I, um, thank you." He took the chilly glass and drained it, head tilted back, throat working as he swallowed. "Mm. Much the best I have had today," he told her. "Thank you for thinking of my comfort."

She hadn't missed the implication. "Somebody else brought you lemonade?"

"Oh, yes," he replied as he finally got his t-shirt straightened out and tugged it back on. "Everyone I have encountered has been uncommonly kind."

I bet. She had finished her mission, but she couldn't tear herself away. "How's the work going?"

"Quite well. These machines, once mastered, make simple work of these kinds of tasks. Though Mrs. Lopez was careful to caution me of their danger, which once begun I could easily see for myself. But I am nearly finished for today, and I have all my fingers and toes." He wiggled the former at her.

She laughed then; she couldn't help it. "Oh, good. I like you with all your parts attached." It was flirty, but she decided to let it stand. It was true, anyway.

Though he returned her smile, his dark eyes widened fractionally. "I—that is—thank you, I believe I should prefer it as well." He cleared his throat, rubbing the back of his neck. "Well—I should finish here, I suppose. I should be home in an hour or so."

"Alright. I'll have dinner ready." She gave him a warm smile and headed back to the house.

Ben watched her go, fully aware that dinner was the farthest thing from his mind while Linnea was in view. The days were warm for so late in the year, and he found that ladies wore much less in public than in his own time—in the case of the woman with the pool, scandalously less: hardly adequate for undergarments, though Mrs. Lopez had only rolled her eyes.

Linnea was never less than appropriate, he thought, watching her golden-brown limbs move gracefully as she crossed the street and went back into their small abode. Though he'd have no objection to seeing *her* clad in a... what was it? Some outlandish word beginning with a B.

Shaking his head, Ben put such unseemly thoughts aside. He was a gentleman, he rebuked himself sharply, and Linnea was his friend and ally. He'd no business wishing for anything... else. He'd no business

174

wishing for anything at all, except a way to get back to Sophia.

Resolutely thrusting everything from his mind except the job at hand, Ben finished the grass and the trimming, received his payment and his sixth glass of lemonade, and bade his employer a good day before heading home—back to Linnea and Kurt's home, he reminded himself abruptly. No matter their kindness, no matter his feelings, this was not his world. As soon as Linnea found that spell, he would have to leave.

In the apartment he headed straight for the shower, both to clean himself and to give himself time to think—and to cool off.

When he emerged once more it was to find delicious smells wafting from the kitchen. Linnea was, for the first time in his memory, wearing a dress. It came down past her knees and had no sleeves, cinched in at the waist by a wide leather belt. She had also pulled her dark hair back in a ponytail and was padding about the kitchen barefoot, humming to herself as she worked over the stove.

His own feet were bare as well, and made little sound on the tiled floor as he came up behind her to peer over her shoulder. "What's all this, then?"

She smiled up at him, dark eyes twinkling. "Dinner. I thought you deserved something nice after all your hard work today. I made paella."

Something in the area of his heart loosened, just a little, at the sight of her sweet face raised to his. "Very nice indeed," he agreed, though he did not look at the stove. "And what is a pi—py—"

"Paella," she pronounced slowly. "It's a Spanish rice dish. This one's got chicken."

Ben watched her mouth as she said the word again, then shook himself. "Sounds wonderful. I confess I am hungry, though I had not looked to find anything that smells quite so delicious as this." Linnea herself, he could not help noticing, was equally delicious, scented with something sweet and cool and refreshing. He tried not to look as though he was sniffing her. "Shall I get us something to drink?" Not lemonade, he hoped, though he had been truthful in telling Linnea he'd preferred hers to the others.

"Sure—in fact, I think there's some red wine on top of the fridge that would go well with this."

He busied himself gathering the glasses and wine. "Will Kurt be joining us?"

"No, he's at work already. It's just us."

A deep wellspring of pleasure bubbled through him at her words, though he tried not to let it show. They'd seen so little of one another over the past week, between her working and his various adventures. Spending time in Linnea's company was something to be savored, to be stored up and remembered, so that when they inevitably parted he could bring out his memories and use them to lend color to his half-toned, drab existence.

"You okay?" Linnea asked him, watching his expression as she served the paella.

Recalling himself to the present moment, Ben smiled and placed a glass of wine by each plate. "Yes, of course." He sipped his wine, then took a bite of the meal she'd made for him, glancing at her in some surprise. "This is delicious!"

She laughed. "I do know how to cook a *few* things," she teased. "I just don't normally take the time."

"Delicious," he repeated. "I have never had the like." He spent a few moments doing justice to the meal, and then spoke as casually as he could manage. "Any luck today?"

"No," she said regretfully, then looked up at him, hesitation in her brown eyes. "I'm going to keep trying, Ben—I want you to know that. I know you're worried about Sophia, and I'm going to try my best to help you get back to her. But... I also want you to know, even if we never find the way to send you back—you have a home here, and friends who love you and will stick by you. We're here for you."

For a moment her face blurred a little; Ben dashed the heel of his hand across his eyes. "Thank you, Linnea," he said quietly. "You—" he flushed and corrected course, "*All* of you have been better friends to me than I could ever have imagined or asked for."

She smiled and reached across the table to take his hand. "You deserve it. You're good people, Ben Fortune."

If she kept this up, he would disgrace himself. Not trusting his voice, Ben gave her a small smile instead and returned his attention to the paella. After a moment to compose himself, he replied in a rough voice, "And you are a remarkable woman, Linnea Santiago. I am so very glad it was you who pulled me from the book, and no other."

Susan and Rose were to join them for dinner the next night. Linnea had decided to make quesadillas, Rose was bringing a casserole, Susan some kind of salad, and Kurt was making cookies. That is, he was putting frozen cookie dough in the oven and taking them out at the right time.

Ben, for his contribution, had decided to make punch using what he called "Prinny's own favored receipt", referring, of course to the Prince Regent that had given his era its name. With some advice from Kurt he'd acquired the correct ingredients, or at least a reasonable facsimile, and was busily measuring and mixing brandy, rum, champagne and various fruit juices in a large pink plastic bowl borrowed from Mrs. Lopez for the purpose.

The cookies were out of the oven and Linnea was about to start on the quesadillas when Susan called. "Lin—I am so sorry," she began, sounding out of breath. "We're going to be later than we thought. Dr. Bialecki has called out of class again, at the last minute. It's just a test I have to proctor, then I'm sending all the little darlings home. Can we push dinner back an hour, or is that a huge hassle?"

"No, that's fine! Come when you can, leave when you must," Linnea replied good-naturedly. "We'll see you then."

"Thank you *so* much! I owe you one. And Bialecki owes *me* one, for this last-minute crap. See you later." A harried-sounding Susan ended the call.

An hour later there was a knock at the door: Susan and Rose, right on time. Linnea opened the door to them. "Welcome, welcome!" As she was hugging Susan hello she caught sight of the white station wagon across the street and down one house. She stiffened.

Susan leaned back to look at her. "What? What is it?"

"That car," Linnea said, dropping her voice even though the inhabitant clearly couldn't hear her from this distance. "It's back…"

Her friend looked around. "What car? What're you talking about?"

"That white station wagon. It's been sitting there off and on for the last couple of weeks. Someone's inside it." Linnea shivered involuntarily. "Do you think they—they know?"

"I don't know how they—wait a minute." Susan's eyes narrowed. "I know that car." So saying, she dumped her bowl of salad in Linnea's arms and stalked toward the white station wagon.

The other four gathered in the doorway to watch with varying degrees of emotion as Susan knocked on the driver's side window, none too gently, and bent to speak to the mysterious occupant within. After a few

179

suspenseful moments, the car door opened and Susan took the driver's arm and escorted her toward the door of the apartment at an implacable march.

"Oh my God," Rose muttered: "it's Bialecki."

Chapter Eleven

Susan ushered a shamefaced Nadine Bialecki into the apartment and closed the door behind her. "Well?" she said, in a tone Linnea was astounded she was using with her adviser. "What's the deal?"

The professor's blush deepened, her gaze continually darting to where Ben stood. "I—I needed to know for sure," she offered, finally. "It *is* him, isn't it? You *are* the real Ben Fortune."

Ben's brows went up at this last question addressed to him. "I am the only Ben Fortune I know, and I am real enough," he temporized with a quick look at Linnea.

Professor Bialecki shook her head. "No. I mean—from the novel. You came out of it, and it changed. And you're here."

Kurt folded his arms. "Do you have any idea how crazy that sounds?"

She rubbed her nose. "Believe me, I do. But... nothing else fits. If he's *not* the real Ben Fortune, then... then how did he come by his information? Nobody else knows, I would stake my reputation on it. I *have* staked my reputation on it."

Susan frowned. "What are you talking about?"

"His name," Bialecki answered, eyes shining. "He said his name was Benoni Jabez Fortune. But how did he know that was Ben Fortune's full name? It's not in the book."

"Then how did *you* know?" Linnea asked, realizing a moment later that her words might be taken as an admission.

"Then it *is* him?" the professor said eagerly. "That's Ben Fortune—Belinda Burnworth's Ben Fortune, made flesh?"

They all looked at one another, unsure whether to admit it or not.

"Then he is," Nadine concluded confidently, nodding.

"But how did you know about the name?" Rose insisted.

Nadine pulled the door open. "Hold on," she replied, but Kurt's big hand was on the door, pushing it shut. "I just need to get something from my car," she insisted.

"Cool." Kurt nodded. "I'll walk you to it, make sure you're safe." He followed the petite woman out onto the sidewalk.

Ben was looking a bit panicky. "How did she know? What can she do to us?"

"We don't know yet that she's going to do anything to us," Susan said, putting a hand on his arm.

"She's always—well, she's always seemed like a really nice person."

Linnea shook her head. That wasn't something they could really count on right now.

A minute later, Dr. Bialecki was hurrying back with a cardboard document box. Her face was absolutely shining with excitement. "A couple of years back I bought some papers in an estate sale in Herefordshire. And you will never *believe* what I found." She opened the box. "Some of Belinda Burnworth's papers. I've had them certified, both as to age and the handwriting. But there was always just a hint of doubt, in the back of my mind. Until I met you." She beamed at Ben.

His expression was doubtful at best. "What have these papers to do with me?"

"Everything," the professor crowed. "Because they're all *about* you. Notes and actual text from the original manuscript for *Fortune's Folly.*" She clapped her hands, for all the world like an excited child. "Undiscovered *canon.*"

Kurt poked one long finger at the papers. "Somebody want to explain, or shall I just go with debonair confusion for now?"

Linnea and Susan had already plunged into the box, so Rose answered. "Canon is the authoritative version of a story and its characters. So the papers give his full name?" she added to Nadine.

"And more," she answered with deep satisfaction. "All about his twin brother, and his relationship with his father and his stepmother, the origin of his nickname—lots of unknown information."

Susan looked up sharply. "And—now that you know that Ben is the real Ben Fortune—what are you planning to do with that knowledge?"

"Do?" Bialecki looked a little blank. "What do you mean?"

"Like, outing him to the media?" Kurt suggested, folding his arms again.

"Of course not!" She seemed genuinely shocked. "I'm just—I'm just delighted to meet you," she said at last, directly to Ben, then to everyone's surprise, dropped a creditable curtsy.

The oven dinged, and everyone looked up. Linnea hesitated a moment. "Would you—like to have dinner with us?" she asked at last. The rules of hospitality were a bit blurry here, but it seemed politic to at least be civil.

Nadine went red again. "I didn't mean—I never intended to intrude," she began, but Ben's manners came to the fore and he offered her his arm.

"If you please, madam." He gave her his best smile, and Linnea wondered if any of the little old ladies at the assisted living facility had actually *survived* meeting him. "I would be most honored if you would join us. I find I am eager to discover for myself all that you have learned."

Dr. Bialecki shifted from red to purple and laid her hand on Ben's arm. "I should be most pleased, sir," she replied in a slightly strangled tone.

Kurt and Rose were already setting another place at the table; the former brought his desk chair from his room to round out the seating, and Ben handed the professor into the squeaky leatherette chair for all the world as if she were royalty, managing to catch the chair before it rolled several feet backward. He got her situated and bowed deeply to her while Kurt quickly stuffed a hamburger bun under the back wheel to prevent the chair from wandering. "Madam," Ben said again with a smile, and took the seat next to her.

Linnea fought down a brief and startling flash of jealousy, and they began passing around the food.

When everyone was served and had taken the edge off their hunger, Linnea asked the question they were all dying to know. "So—this original manuscript. What's it like?"

Dr. Bialecki's eyes lit up. "It's *hilarious*. I was disposed to be offended at first, because I've always loved Araminta as a character, and the original story makes fun of her—it's a satire." Ben began choking on his wine, as though he'd inhaled it rather than swallowed. Nadine went on, oblivious, as Linnea patted Ben's back. "But it really is funny. It's an epistolary novel, so Araminta writes these letters telling how she saw events, and then you get a letter from another person showing how wrong she is about everything. Several of the letters are written by you," she added to Ben.

"My letters to Sophia—you have them?"

"Yes—all about your first meeting with Araminta, and the incident with the supposedly narrowly-missed proposal…"

"But wait," Susan broke in. "If the original novel's so funny, why did Burnworth change it?"

"She lent it to a couple of friends to read, and they loved Ben Fortune so much that they wanted the romance to be sincere. It was late enough in the Regency that that kind of broad satire was on its way out—they wanted romance and sincerity. So Burnworth reluctantly changed the story. A lot of it's still there, though, if you look. The scenes are based on Araminta's point of view, and a lot of them are transposed almost directly from her letters. It's just that we never get Fortune's side of the story."

"Then that is why—" he began, then broke off suddenly.

"Why what?" Kurt asked.

"Why I recall some events with such clarity and others not at all, though I might be supposed to do so," came the slow reply. "I have wondered… there was so much about me that was not in the book. And yet I could remember facets of my—my character," he winced slightly, "that I knew were true, though they ought not to have existed."

"So did the papers change just like the novel?" Rose asked as Kurt got up to fetch the cookies.

"Yes!" Dr. Bialecki bounced in her chair and the hamburger bun slowly flattened. "That's how I know it's canon! Because nothing noncanonical changed, you know. The film script hasn't changed, so it's not authoritative—it's not true to the original."

"And neither did the fanfiction!" Linnea added. Nadine's excitement was contagious.

"Exactly! But all the full versions of the text, both hardcopy and digital—and audio, actually—*did* change. And so did the original manuscript. Some of Mr. Fortune's later letters disappeared entirely, in fact. But not the earlier ones, like that delightful one about 'prunes and prisms' that Burnworth wrote about to a friend and that eventually got referred to in Dickens."

Ben looked completely unnerved. "Then—despite the lack of her mention in the current novel, my sister does still exist," he finally said, his voice strained. "I had worried that my exit might have—but my memories were so clear, I hoped—prayed—excuse me for a moment, please." He got up with alacrity and went into Kurt's room, closing the door.

They all looked at one another. After a moment, Linnea picked up Ben's glass and went to knock quietly on the door.

There was a pause, and then: "Come in." Ben sat upon Kurt's bed, his head in his hands. He didn't look up. "I am sorry to interrupt the party," he rasped, his voice low. "It's just—this is not academic, to me."

"I know, sweetie," she said, setting the glass on the desk. She sat down next to him and put her arms around him. He leaned into her embrace wordlessly.

Linnea pressed her cheek to his curls and held him for a while in silence. It felt so—so right. Not that he was upset, but that she was there to comfort him, and that he would let her with such trust. This was what she had wanted to do almost since she had met him: be a friend to him—be *more* than a friend to him—

There was a knock at the door and Susan poked her head in. "Ben—there's something you should read."

"What is it?" he asked, and Linnea could read stark fear in his dark eyes.

Susan held out a fragile-looking document. "When those other letters disappeared, this one appeared," she told him. "It's from Sophia. To you."

He took it in trembling hands, looking about for his reading glasses. Linnea found them on the bedside table. "Shall I leave you to it?" she asked softly as Susan withdrew.

"No—please stay." His gaze was imploring. "You little know what comfort I take in your presence."

She nodded and settled in next to him as he cleared his throat and began to read aloud.

"*Ben, O, my Ben,*" it began, "*tell me it is not true—come through that door this instant and tell me it was all a mistake, a joke, a lie, a rumor! Tell me you have not gone where it would be a sin for me to follow, and left me to Uncle Moribund. My heart cries that you must be somewhere; but you see I no longer ask for my letters to be franked, for I would only be told that you cannot be found.*

"*When once Uncle Moribund deposed with the solicitors that you had gone, my guardianship was given to him. He left me here, with Miss Guillefoyle, until the*

188

quarter was paid out; and now I am to have no season, but am already to be wed, to a Captain Yarrow. He cared not for a dowry, wanted a young, strong bride to take to India—the younger the better, I heard him say so to Uncle Moribund, though why that should be funny I cannot think.

"I suppose, now you are truly gone, that it does not much matter where I go, as you will never be there again. How shall I live without your counsel and good humor? To what standard must I now measure my acquaintance? —for you were all I held to be right, and good, and dear.

"O my dear brother, if you could but return to me, I should face any other hardship with good cheer; but this loss, I confess, is too much for my poor soul to bear.

"They tell me that you are in God's keeping now, and for your sake I will believe it, and try to live as well as I can, that I might someday join you beyond this Earthly plane. O Ben, think of me sometimes, and know that I shall never forget you, if I live to be ninety. Your own, Sophia," he finished, his voice breaking. He turned a haunted countenance upon Linnea. "I must get back," he whispered. "I must! There must be a way!"

She nodded. "We'll keep looking. I promise. Here—" She handed him his glass.

Ben pushed it away. "No, I thank you. I have not the leisure to spare. I am resolved. If mortal thought will find this spell, then I shall not rest until it is found." His gaze softened a little as he looked at her. "You have

189

worked on my behalf for weeks, and I have allowed you to do it without regard nor recompense, because…" He shook his head. "No, I shall not dissemble. You deserve the truth. I… *like* it here. Perhaps too much. And I shall miss you, when I am gone." His chin lifted. "But go I must."

Linnea wanted to stop him, to keep him from going. It was selfish of her, she knew that—but he couldn't go, not yet, not when she had just realized—not when she felt—

Luckily, pragmatic considerations were on her side. "But how are we going to find the spell? That archive is huge—and maybe the spell's not even there! Maybe it doesn't exist!"

This time it was Kurt's dark head that peeked in on them. "You guys okay in here?"

"Yes," Ben responded, rubbing at his eyes. "Forgive me, please. It was rude of me to leave so precipitously."

"Don't worry about that," his friend told him. "Take all the chill you need. We're just going through papers out here, no big." Kurt raised an interrogative brow at Linnea.

"We'll help you," Linnea said, taking Ben's hand.

When they reemerged, everyone was gathered around the box on the coffee table. Ben cleared his throat. "Any new discoveries?" he asked, with a feeble attempt at heartiness.

Nadine stood up. "Mr. Fortune," she began, "I want to apologize—please believe that I never meant to upset you. I'd been thinking of the story, and not of how all this must weigh on you. If I've caused you distress, I am truly sorry."

He nodded, his lips quirking as though he was trying to smile. "Think not on it, Dr. Bialecki. My shoulders are broad enough for such cares. And while my sister's fate does worry me, it is better to have some information than none at all; for that I thank you from my heart."

"Um..." Susan held something up. "There's worse, Ben." Her face was pale as she handed the letter to him.

Linnea watched as all the color drained from Ben's face. "Worse?" he managed, and took the letter. "*My dearest brother,*" he began shakily, then cleared his throat and began again. "*My dearest brother,*

"*I pray you will forgive me for what I am about to do. There is no one to help me, nothing left for me—indeed, nothing left of me, and I can see only one way to peace, though I risk the wrath of God himself...*" Ben's voice went on sudden hiatus, brows snapping down as he read the page rapidly, then read it again, a muscle clenching in his jaw.

"What?" Linnea read over his shoulder, her eyes widening as she went. "That—that *bastard!*" she spat.

Ben let the letter fall back into the box; Rose snatched it up. "Oh my God," she muttered, her eyes darting back and forth as she read. "That poor girl—

Yarrow never married her," she told an avid Kurt and Dr. Bialecki in an undertone with a quick glance at Ben. He turned his back on the group as Rose hurried on. "He—er—*ruined* her," she said meaningly. "She thought they *were* married, but it was a sham, to save money on the expense of a license. Moribund Fortune paid him her dowry—and then on the ship to India Yarrow introduced her as his—um—" Rose winced. "Paid companion, and invited the other men to…" She dropped the letter like it had burned her fingers. "Ben, I'm so—"

"Do not apologize to me," he said without turning. "*Help* me. None of this would have happened had I been there to protect her—none of it *will* happen, if I can only get back!"

"Well, why don't you bring *her* out?" Nadine asked. "You managed to bring him out, why not her?"

There was a pause as they considered this. "That was an accident," Kurt said slowly, thinking through the implications. "We had no control over any of it—he just came from a random part of the book." He was silent for a moment. "We could try it, but—there's no guarantee we'd get her early enough. Or even… alive."

Ben's shoulders shook, once. Linnea put her hand on his arm. "I just—I don't know what else to do!" she said helplessly. "I've been looking through John Key's papers to see if he found a spell to send characters back, but I've found next to nothing. There's just so much material, and no guarantee the spell even exists!"

"Now, wait." Nadine held up her hand, brows drawn together over top of her glasses. "I spoke to Jack Helman about you, when I…" Her cheeks colored lightly. "When I found out where Mr. Fortune was living. I asked him what you were doing for your diss, and off he went on his hobbyhorse—as I suppose we are all wont to do, given the right provocation." She hunched her shoulders slightly. "At any rate, he mentioned—isn't there a tale that Key once brought a character out of a book at a dinner party, and then sent the character back?" Linnea nodded, slowly, and the professor went on. "So the spell must exist. That's not the kind of story somebody would make out of whole cloth, especially since we know the first spell *does* exist."

"Yeah, but how does that help me find the second in that huge archive?" Linnea asked.

"Well—you could talk to Jack Helman," Nadine suggested. "Ask him where the dinner party story comes from. Maybe there'll be some clues in it."

Linnea paused for a moment, her stomach dropping suddenly like she'd taken the express elevator to the top of the Space Needle. The story, widely considered apocryphal, wasn't a part of the archive. It had been written by someone else, a contemporary of Janky's, so it hadn't crossed her radar. But in retrospect it was… an absolutely *brilliant* idea. "Why didn't I think of that?" she asked at last. *Because you didn't really want to find the answer*, that mocking voice in her head replied. She silenced it, hard, gritting her teeth. Her own feelings didn't enter into this. She needed to do this—for Ben.

Ben was watching her, his black eyes nearly burning a hole in her. "This Dr. Helman—he is your adviser, as Dr. Bialecki is Susan's, correct? I have heard you mention the name. If he can help—" He clenched his jaw. "Expose me as you must: I invite any scrutiny, any loss, if it will only save my sister."

"I don't think that's going to be necessary, Linnea assured him, her mind racing. "I've got this."

Dr. Helman was notoriously difficult to schedule anything with... unless you knew which buttons to push. Linnea left him a voicemail that pushed them without mercy.

"I'm so glad to hear you've found such a fascinating topic for your dissertation!" he praised her in his office, first thing the next morning. "Key's famous dinner party and the source of the story—wonderful!"

"Yeah," Linnea answered as enthusiastically as she could, taking a seat by his desk. "The only thing is—I've never actually read that account of his dinner party. I've heard it referred to, but…" She shrugged. "I don't know where to find it."

"Oh, you can read it on the Eighteenth Century Correspondence Database!" he answered, opening his laptop and hitting keys. Linnea came around the desk to watch over his shoulder. He accessed the database through the university library website, and in a few moments was typing the name of the author, one Hezekiah Pym, into the search bar. In less than a minute he found the right letter, downloaded the PDF, emailed it to Linnea, and printed out a copy for her.

"Dr. Helman, you are a *lifesaver*," Linnea gushed.

He preened slightly. "I have lots of ideas for ways you could go with this—"

"That's great!" she answered, refusing to take the hint and grabbing her bag. "I'll set up another meeting with you after I've read this, shall I? Great talking with you—thanks again!" She was out in the hall on the word and hurrying toward the library. She fired off a group text as she went: *Got the letter! En route to archive.*

A moment later, her phone buzzed in response: from Kurt. Or no, Linnea realized as she opened it. From Ben, on Kurt's phone, evidently. *If an answer is to be found, I know you will find it. Bless you. ~B*

Linnea smiled a little painfully and hurried toward the elevator.

The letter was given both as a scan of the original, and in a typed transcription. Linnea sat down at her desk and pored over the typed version.

...I have recently had a most diverting experience. My dear, you will not credit the tale, but I swear by God and all his holy angels that I shall tell you truly. We were invited to dine with John Key, a philosopher of some note and a favorite of Mrs.

Fitzherbert. Eliza claimed a headache, as she did not wish to be associated with any acquaintance of That Lady; for myself, I accepted, as society makes fewer demands of delicacy among my sex, and I confess to overwhelming curiosity about the man who wrote so eloquently upon such a prosaic subject as the mangle-wurzel and still commanded the attention of the Court.

Nor was I disappointed. The conversation was most lively, though I shall not bore you with most of it, for I know well your tastes, dear sister, and I know too, from long experience, not to seek your rebuke for boredom. Therefore I will tell you... " Linnea's eyes glazed over as Pym went into excruciating detail about the decor, the dress of each personage assembled, their bearing and temperament and... aha!

...It being the sixth evening after Michaelmas, the air was crisp and clear, that being the very best weather for the harvest of root vegetables, in particular parsnips, of which you know I am uncommonly fond. I wish you will find Lewes' old receipt for the roasted parsnips which we used to... She skimmed ahead. *... and so Mr. Key described his theory of the reality behind invented universes, to wit: that every novel carries within it the potential to become as real as you or I.*

You can imagine the skepticism with which this claim was received. The words 'utter nonsense' and 'imbecilic twaddle' were thrown about without recourse to common courtesy. And rightly so, you may think, and so I will confess did I, until he proved his point.

I know you will want to know how he did it, and I cannot rightly say. He produced a green commonplace book and read words that bade the man appear: Tristram Shandy, in the flesh, I swear it. An actor, you will say, and I cannot blame you for thinking this all a pantomime, or an elaborate joke upon my part; but I swear to you, Caro, may God strike me dead if I did not witness the man appear! One moment he was not there, the next he was among us, wild-eyed and terrified, begging to know whether 'twas some kind of fever from which he could not awake. After some moments in which we questioned him as to his identity, Key took pity upon the distraught soul and returned him to the pages from whence he sprang. Now *what think you of my London sojourn?*

A green commonplace book. Linnea had seen quite a number of them in the archives. But which one?

She sat thinking for a moment. It was a mystery: a research mystery. She needed clues. What other clues could she get from the letter?

The date. She checked: the letter was written in May of 1766. That meant that Janky had created and written down the spell in a green commonplace book before that date. It might even be close to that date: Janky might have been showing off his most recent discovery.

Alright. Find May 1766 and work backwards.

The papers tended to be in a *somewhat* chronological order: it seemed that Janky had just stacked them away as he went, like soil layers, and when they had been put into boxes they had retained something of their chronology. Linnea began searching boxes.

It took quite a while. It was late afternoon by the time she found 1766, and began flipping through.

She came up with three green commonplace books in a row. Well, it was somewhere to start, anyway.

In the end, she searched through five commonplace books before she found it. There it was, plain and clear: no manicules, no codes, just the spell and a shit-ton of instructions.

She stared at it for a long moment. *You could put that back on a shelf,* a little voice said. *You could hide it so well in this damned archive that no one would ever find it again.*

Linnea took a deep breath. *Love is not self-seeking,* she remembered her mother reading to her. *It always protects, always trusts, always hopes, always perseveres.* She stuffed the notebook in her bag with a painful sort of triumph and texted to everyone with trembling fingers: *I FOUND IT.*

Chapter Twelve

Ben's fingers were shaking as he tied his cravat for the fifth—sixth?—time. It was now officially a wrinkled mess, which seemed appropriate for his feelings, if not to the salons of the *Ton*.

The message had come from Linnea not this quarter-hour past, and while Kurt had done something he called a 'victory lap' around the apartment, Ben had dashed to their shared room to don his own clothing, so that he might be ready to go as soon as might be, and to damnation with his conflicting feelings. Sophia was what mattered now, not this strange desolation at the idea of not seeing… certain friends again.

With something approaching a growl, he jerked off the cravat and began anew. He'd had a life these few weeks, a real life in the real world, which was more than he ought to have had, more than anyone of his fictional acquaintance would ever have, and the memory of it—of her—would have to suffice.

And yet he knew, with conviction deep as his soul, that the memory of golden-brown eyes and skin and dark hair, combined with the knowledge that he would not experience the quiet joy of being in Linnea's company again, would leave him a lesser man. She made him better; she made him want to learn more and give more and *be* more, and without her he would simply be bereft.

But he was not born for this world—in truth he had not been *born* at all, only sprung full-grown from the mind of a middle-aged spinster and displayed a veneer of existence for the pleasure of others. Though he *felt* real enough, as did Sophia. And he could no more abandon her to their uncle's abuse than he could saw off his own leg.

Ben shook his head, finally satisfied with his cravat. Enough circular thinking. Enough *feeling*. His course was clear; to wish otherwise was an exercise in futility.

He heard the front door open, heard Kurt greet Linnea, shouting something about a 'five high,' and his heart was like to pound out of his chest. Ben swallowed once, ran a hand over his hair, and went to meet his fate.

Linnea greeted him with a brave smile, her brown eyes warm and affectionate, and all his resolve to remain stoic fled, along with any sense of propriety. Instead he caught her up in his arms, holding her tightly. "Bless you—thank you—I can never—you are so—" he tried and then gave up and simply pressed his mouth to hers, kissing her with abandon.

"Well, okay then." Ben barely registered Kurt in the background as the other man slunk into his room and shut the door.

At last reason returned; Ben lifted his head and looked down to see Linnea's expression: it was rather dazed and glassy. Lord, what had he done? He sprang back from her like a scalded cat. "Linnea—forgive me, I did not mean—" And that was a lie, for he'd meant every second of it. But he'd never intended to startle her, or frighten her, or compromise their friendship, which was of more value to him than he could express. He took refuge in formality, bowing slightly. "My deepest apologies, Miss Santiago. I quite forgot myself, and would not so importune you for the world. Pray do not let it distress you unduly—I swear to you it will not happen again."

"Wh—uh—But—"

Ben held up a hand. "I beg you will not speak of it, and nor shall I. Now, tell me of your discovery, if you will."

From the bedroom came a muffled shout. "Is it safe to come out or should I plan to be in here a while?" which was immediately followed by unseemly cackling.

Ben's face was afire with humiliation as a grinning Kurt came out of his room without waiting for a reply. "You could just shoot me, it would be quicker," Ben muttered as his friend shouldered past him and spread himself all over the sofa like butter on a large plaid scone.

Kurt was still grinning like a lunatic, all his teeth showing. "So what'dja find?" he asked Linnea, who had dropped everything on the floor.

"Uh—" She still looked a little stunned, but she managed to pull herself together and retrieved her bag. "Well, I got the notebook. It's all in here—and not in code, either." She was sounding more like herself by the moment.

Which somehow only made Ben feel even guiltier. He cleared his throat, resisting the urge to run his finger around the inside of his collar. "And will it work, do you think?"

"Only one way to find out." She didn't look at him. "There are a lot of instructions, though—I need to read them first." She perched on the edge of the couch and opened the notebook.

"Do you—may I offer assistance?" Dismay flooded him, though he could not tell whether it was due more to her avoidance of his gaze or the realization that his departure would not be immediate.

"No, I got it." She looked up to give him a quick smile. "Just give me a bit. You know what Janky's handwriting is like."

Relief replaced despair and suddenly Ben could breathe again. She had forgiven him for his lapse of decorum, it seemed, though he could little forgive himself. Kurt, meanwhile, was watching the two of them as though at some sort of sporting match: first one then the other, back and forth, grin firmly in place. "We not gonna talk about this?" he asked, and Ben could cheerfully have sat on him for it.

"No, we are not," he said icily. "If you are burning to be useful, perhaps you could make some of your cookies, for when Miss S—when *Linnea,*" he corrected himself conscientiously, "needs a break."

"Seriously?" Kurt shrugged. "Alright, man. Cookies it is." He folded himself up and rolled into the kitchen, his gait easy.

Linnea looked up again. "It's okay," she said quietly, with another small smile, and then bent over the commonplace book once more, taking notes as she went.

Ben could settle to nothing. He paced, he fidgeted, he thought about brewing himself a cup of tea with those horrible little bags, all the while trying not to think about her soft lips against his, how she'd seemed to respond for a moment before rational thought returned. Yet the taste and feel of Linnea was now imprinted on him like a brand, and he realized that while he somehow knew *how* to kiss a woman—for would not every Regency buck? —he, Ben, had never truly *done* it before. Like playing chess. He had never kissed Araminta, that was certain. And for him, in the novel, there was no one else.

And never would be.

He headed for the kitchen. Tea, definitely. And by tea he meant brandy.

Linnea came in some time later. "Okay! I've got it." She was smiling, looking much more cheerful than she had before, and his heart sank. Likely now she was glad to see the back of him. Still, he tried to respond in kind.

"I had every faith you would," he told her, finishing his brandy and straightening his coat. "I am ready, though I should like to say goodbye to the others, if Kurt will lend me his phone for a moment."

"Oh, they should be over soon." Linnea put the commonplace book and her notes on the kitchen table. "Here's the deal. This spell was actually made for rea— nonfictional people to enter books," she corrected herself quickly, with a side-glance at Ben. "But there's no reason it shouldn't work for you—and I think it's what Janky used to send poor Tristram Shandy back, anyway. And boy, does that explain a lot about *that* novel," she added, shaking her head. "This spell is clearly more advanced than the other one. Janky really must've figured some stuff out in between. For example, you can choose where and when in the story you go back to. So we can make sure you get in there before anything happens to Sophia."

Ben could actually feel weight lifting from his shoulders. "Thank God," he breathed.

"*And*," Linnea added, her smile broadening irrepressibly, "the other good news is that, since this spell was made for non-fictional people to enter books... there's a way back out again."

His mouth dropped open. "What are you saying?"

"I'm saying," she said, grinning, "that when you've got Sophia, you can bring her back out. You don't have to stay."

His very skin prickled, the pit of his stomach plummeting much as it had done when on the escalator at the library. "I can—we can come back? Here? And you—you would not object?"

Kurt broke in just as the doorbell rang. "Mind? Aw, hell, Ben—things wouldn't be the same without you."

He went to answer the door, and Linnea reached over and pressed Ben's arm. "Please come back," she said softly.

From nadir to apex in one giant leap. Ben felt lightheaded. A life—a real life—for him and for Sophia. Impulsively he grasped both Linnea's hands. "I will, I promise."

There might have been more to say, but the apartment was now filled with people, and so he let her go.

"So you really have it?" Susan hurried into the kitchen, Nadine on her heels.

"Yep!" Linnea laughed. "Now we have to figure out where and when Ben is going to return to. Oh," she added, turning back to him, "and you need to memorize the return spell. When you say it, you need to be touching everything you want to bring back with you—and *only* what you want to bring back. No Uncle Andrew and the cab horse, please. You'll have to hold Sophia's hand."

He looked at her in some bemusement. "My uncle's name is Morbiund, but I take your point. I shall memorize it diligently."

"Okay—here." She handed him her notes and pointed out the spell. "It's pretty short, so memorizing it shouldn't be too hard. And we'll figure out where and when we need to send you back to."

Nadine had already been considering this question, and after much consulting of the dates on Sophia's tragic letters and the events of Araminta's narrative, they established the correct page, location, and date for Ben's return: London, a day or so before Sophia's arrival. "It is likely I would miss her on the post road," he agreed. "And this gives me time to confront my uncle about his perfidy and intercept my sister before she ever learns of his terrible machinations."

"Excellent! Well—are you all ready? Got your handkerchief?" Linnea teased.

He pretended to be affronted, drawing himself up, raising a brow at her. "Naturally." In truth he was drinking her in, memorizing her in these last moments, just in case Key's spell or his memory should fail him.

"And you have the spell memorized?" she added, pinning him with a Look that he strongly suspected was meant to imitate his own.

"I do." Ben couldn't help the smile that broke through his put-on demeanor, tapping his temple. "Good student, remember?"

"Of course." She paused a moment, then threw her arms around him. "Be careful, okay?" she said into his waistcoat.

He held her close for longer than he ought, then reluctantly let her go. "If I don't return," he began, "I want you all to know—"

"You *better* freaking return," Susan interrupted. "And if you don't, we're sending in the cavalry."

Ben chuckled and, with his finger on the correct page of *Fortune's Folly*, lifted his chin and repeated John Key's spell. "This day of April, London, please," he added.

And winked out of existence, just like that.

Chapter Thirteen

Linnea took a deep breath and sat down, feeling lightheaded. It was one thing *knowing* that was going to happen; it was another thing entirely to *watch* it.

"You okay?" Kurt asked.

Linnea silently reached a hand out. He gave her the plate of cookies, and she stuffed one in her mouth.

Everyone seemed sobered by Ben's disappearance. Linnea ate cookie after cookie, waiting for him to reappear.

Nothing happened.

"Why isn't he back yet?" she finally asked, and heard her voice become high with stress.

Susan shook her head. "Maybe it takes some time—maybe he has to reconnect with Araminta, since the novel's in her point of view? Or maybe it has to do with the sheer volume of what needs to change? As I recall, the changes to *Fortune's Folly* weren't immediate the last time, either—you said he showed up at your place the night before, and it was overnight that the changes started registering."

Rose picked up the novel and began scanning the pages. "I don't see any changes yet."

"Oh, God, I hope they don't happen in real time," Linnea groaned, then suddenly put down the plate of cookies with a clatter. "You know what? I'm going to bed. Watched pots never boil, and I can't handle watching this one. Night, guys. Thank you." She fled to her room.

But not to sleep. She turned out the lights, but tossed and turned for what seemed like eons, imagining all sorts of horrible scenarios. When at last she did fall asleep, it was to fitful dreams filled with vaguely threatening figures, and she woke frequently.

At five in the morning she fell into a deeper sleep from sheer exhaustion, and awoke to Kurt, banging on her door. "Lin—Lin, wake up! It's happening!"

"Mmm. Go 'way," she muttered. Memory struck, and she sat straight up. "What? What is it?" she asked in alarm.

Her door opened and Kurt came in, still in what passed for his pajamas, his laptop open to a noisy news channel. He clambered onto her bed, ignoring her protests when he kneed her in the stomach. "Just shut up and look, will you?"

The video he was streaming showed a woman in front of the omnipresent backdrop of Tom Hattleson's determined glare, and the banner headline: *Ben Fortune Returns?* The anchor was speaking breathlessly as a video feed played over her. "Here we have actual footage of the book changing, morphing, if you will, right before a stunned reader's eyes. How this is being accomplished, and to what end, no one can say for sure."

The video had apparently been taken on a cell phone, and sure enough, the text on the page was changing. The clip was short, and they played it over and over again. "For those just tuning in, Ben Fortune has returned to the novel *Fortune's Folly*. Some are calling this a blatant advertisement for the upcoming movie, a theory which the producers strongly denied at a press conference this morning."

The shot changed to a long table with a number of middle-aged white men sitting behind it, flashbulbs going off constantly in their faces. "We have nothing to do with the changing text of Belinda Burnworth's nineteenth-century classic," one man announced firmly. "We are as astonished as everyone else, and watching breathlessly to see what will happen next. Fans of the novel can be assured that the film will follow the original version."

The shot changed to people lining up to purchase copies at large chain bookstores. "Sales have gone through the roof as people wish to watch the text changing for themselves. Some are calling this a brilliant strategy in interactive reading. Others are calling it a mystery on the scale of the Loch Ness Monster and the Bermuda triangle."

People were picketing, with signs that read *Bring Back Burnworth* and *Down With This Sort of Thing!* "It seems that Araminta Cavanaugh, the heroine of *Fortune's Folly*, has just attended a card party in

210

Chapter Ten, at which she has been assured by a reliable source that Ben Fortune has returned to town and has been seen hurrying into his uncle's house. No more information is available at this time, but fans of the novel are waiting with bated breath for further changes."

Linnea let out a breath she didn't know she'd been holding. "So he's gotten there all right," she said.

"Looks like," her roommate agreed. "Listen, I've got an early call at the ER today. You got this okay?"

"Yeah." She rubbed at her eyes, which felt like they were full of sand. "I'll manage. Thanks."

"Okay." He patted her shoulder. "You text me if you need me—or even have me paged if you need to. I'll tell 'em it's a family emergency." Kurt climbed back over her, dropping a kiss on her forehead as he went. "It's going to be fine, Lin. You'll see. He'll be back before dinner."

She gave him a tight smile, and got out of bed. No way was she going to be able to sleep any more *now*.

She showered, made herself breakfast, and then sat on the couch with her laptop and tried to pretend nothing important was happening. It was a mostly unsuccessful endeavor. Bumblr was full of discussions of *Fortune's Folly*, and so were all the news sites: the twenty-four-hour news cycle was having absolute fits. She managed to distract herself for a while playing some card games, and finally logged onto Faceplace.

And that's when she saw it on her feed: *FORTUNE'S FATALITY*, the headline on a linked article read. *BEN FORTUNE DIES.*

Linnea stared at it for a moment in undiluted horror, then clicked on the link. *In the ever-changing text of 'Fortune's Folly,'* the article declared, *Ben Fortune is now reported to be dead.*

"Terrible News," Aunt Virulea declared in capital letters the next morning when Araminta went down to breakfast. *"It appears we must cross Mr. Fortune from our list of marital candidates forever. Such a pity,"* she added with a sigh: *"so wealthy a young man."*

"What do you mean, Aunt?" Araminta asked in alarm.

"Why—this," Aunt Virulea answered, sliding the newspaper over to her trembling niece. *"MR. B— F— OF HEREFORDSHIRE SLAIN,"* it read. *"It has come to the attention of the editors of this paper that the handsome Mr. B— F—, nicknamed 'Devil,' was found brutally beaten this morning in an alley not far from his town house. It seems most likely he was set upon by footpads. Mr. B— F— set all the Town talking when he suddenly disappeared from his Herefordshire estate some weeks ago. He was seen in London yesterday, at the home of his uncle, Mr. M— F—. It is still unknown to the editors of this paper where Mr. B— F— hid*

himself during those mysterious few weeks." The paper
fell from Araminta's nerveless fingers.

Linnea sat back, staring at her screen in disbelief, feeling like someone had punched her in the gut. Ben was... dead? Her mind shied away from the idea. No. No! He couldn't be dead. He couldn't! She scrubbed at her eyes, trying to see the webpage through a sudden film of blurry tears. She couldn't leave it like this. There had to be—surely there was something she could do? She could use the original spell—pull him out of the novel again—

But then what if it pulled him out too early and he didn't know her? Oh, God, what a mess. Linnea dropped her face into her hands with a groan.

Then she straightened up again. The second spell. Maybe she couldn't pull Ben out of the book again—but *she* could go in to *him*. All she had to do was go in before he was killed. And if she caught those footpads...

Linnea felt a wave of pure rage wash over her. She snapped her laptop shut and marched into Kurt's room, returning in a few moments with the aluminum baseball bat he kept in his closet. She pulled out Key's notebook and the novel and worked out where and when she wanted to go.

She would have to tell Kurt what was happening. She grabbed a piece of paper, jotted down a short note, and stuck it by the novel. Then, with the bat in one hand

213

and the other finger holding her spot in the novel, she declaimed the spell in a firm voice, specifying where and when she wanted to land.

A moment later, the apartment was empty, but for the sound of rustling pages.

Linnea stared around in surprise. Regency London, she had been prepared for: no electric lights, the sound and smell of horses, night watchmen calling that all was well. What she had *not* been prepared for was... nothing.

Fictional Regency London was... gray. Gray and formless, almost as if it were constructed entirely of fog. Sights, sounds, and smells were alike fuzzy and indeterminate. But she knew she was on the pavement by a street, that there were houses and very few street lamps—and that a figure was walking toward her in the darkness.

She slipped into the gray shadow of a gray townhouse and waited. A familiar figure approached in his blue coat and buff breeches. As he came nearer things grew more distinct, as if he carried color and detail with him: the pavement was harder, the air less thick, the darkness less impenetrable.

Linnea let Ben pass—and sure enough, two menacing, shadowy figures followed behind him.

She stepped out behind them. "Hey!" she barked. All three wheeled to stare at her as she gritted her teeth and swung, and a moment later there was a satisfying, musical *PONNNG* from the bat and one footpad lay groaning on the ground.

"L—Linnea?" Ben stuttered, then seemed to take in the situation, black brows snapping downward as he doubled his fists in the approved 'Gentleman Jackson' style. "What are you doing here?" he hissed, squaring off with the other footpad.

"THIS," she answered, lip curling as she swung for the outfield. *PONNNG.*

Ben stared, nonplussed, as the second man went down like a rock. He dropped his fists and looked at her. "But—what—"

She stepped over the groaning, indefinite, human-shaped lumps on the ground, which were currently trying to crawl away from the brightly-colored Linnea and her all-too-real metal bat. She grabbed the back of his head and pulled him down to kiss him, hard, on the lips.

He made a sound of astonishment that smoothed out into pleasure as his arms went about her, holding her tightly. "Linnea," he rasped as their lips parted briefly, then met again.

Someone cleared her throat. Nobody cared. "Excuse me," someone said, and then "EXCUSE ME." A small body interposed itself between them, shoving none too gently.

"Dr. Bialecki?" Ben mumbled, dazed.

"Yes," Nadine replied shortly, her eyes snapping. "Kindly control yourselves long enough for privacy, unless you want to be arrested for indecent behavior. And put this on," she added to Linnea, shoving a bundle of sprigged muslin at her. "*Honestly*," she added with a shake of her head, clearly exasperated. "And after that display, if anyone asks, you're married."

Linnea felt suddenly giddy. "He's seen me with my hair down and touched my bare leg. I think by Regency standards we've been married for a couple of weeks," she giggled.

Nadine gave her a Look that was worthy of Ben, while Ben himself flushed with deep color. "Dress. On. Now. Honestly," she repeated, as Linnea handed her bat to Ben and pulled the gown over her t-shirt and jeans. "All it took was two hours and a couple of phone calls to borrow some stuff from the drama department, but nooo. You had to give us all a heart attack. Hello, Ben," she added with a friendly smile. "Having a safe evening? Good. I'm heading back to the modern world. Now both of you hurry off to Ben's townhouse. Tell the servants you're married, or it'll be all over Town." She gave them each a shove in the small of the back. "AND NO PDA," she added as they hurried away.

"PDA?" Ben asked, bemused.

"Public Displays of Affection." Linnea took Ben's arm with one hand, still holding the baseball bat with the other. She tucked it under her elbow like a riding crop. "So have you caught up with Sophia yet?" she asked brightly, still full of delight at seeing him again and knowing he was all right.

He was looking down at her with the dazed and thrilled expression of a man who has just discovered a true fortune. "No, she is still on the road from Bath. Linnea, how did you—why—?"

"The book changed," she explained. "And it—" He needed to know, but she didn't want to tell him. "It said you were killed by footpads. I couldn't let that happen."

"K—killed?" He swallowed, seeming to need a moment to process that. "Who would..." His face hardened. "My uncle grows desperate, I gather." And then he looked at her again, and his handsome face settled into lines of utter besottedness. "You came to save me."

"Of course I did," she answered. "I love you, Ben. Of course I came."

He stopped dead in his tracks, turned to face her, taking her by the upper arms as he searched her face. "You—Linnea, you—love me?" His dark eyes were alight; he leaned toward her, before recalling that they were in public. "Bloody hell. I love you, too."

She smiled and hugged him quickly with her free arm. "I know. You wouldn't have kissed me like that when I came home if you didn't."

Ben rubbed the back of his neck. "I wish I'd known," he muttered, then looked up. "Here—my house in Town." He led her up a set of broad white steps and through a heavy, arched door. No sooner had it slammed behind them before she was in his arms, his mouth seeking hers.

The bat dropped to the floor with a musical clunk and she was kissing him back, her arms around his neck, probably getting far more enthusiastic than any lady in the Regency era would be caught dead doing.

And caught they were. For the second time that night, someone cleared his throat. "Sir."

Again Ben leapt away from Linnea as though burnt. "Oh *hell*—er, hello, Strathmore." As he spoke, the indistinct gray figure before them resolved into a Regency-era butler, complete with silver salver and supercilious expression.

Linnea bit her lip and tried not to smile.

"Good evening, Sir," Strathmore answered, pretending he had seen nothing.

Ben pinched the bridge of his nose, took a breath, and spoke with the air of a man taking a leap. "Strathmore: my wife, Mrs. Fortune. Please have her chambers prepared immediately." After a minute hesitation, the butler bowed and glided away, presumably to carry out his master's orders. Ben took a deep breath. "That will be all over the *Ton* before morning. Will you mind?" he asked Linnea.

She smiled irrepressibly. "Kiss me again."

"Oh, you *darling*," he murmured, and pulled her into his arms. She liked that mode of address, and let him know it.

All too soon Strathmore was back, though he had the air of having given them a bit of time alone as an indulgence. "Will you be having supper, Madam?"

Linnea had expected him to address Ben, and was surprised. But she was hungry. "Yes, please, Strathmore. It—needn't be fancy." The poor cook…

218

He merely bowed in response, and faded away again. Ben watched him go, a bemused expression on his face.

"What is it?" Linnea asked.

"It's…" He shook his head as though clearing it. "It just occurs to me to wonder whether I actually *have* a cook. I've never seen him, of that I am sure."

Linnea chuckled. "I'm sure many nonfictional Regency gentlemen saw their cooks very infrequently. As long as the phantom cook produces food, I don't care."

Ben was still a bit abstracted. "I can't think how I never saw it before, the way everything—even Strathmore—is gray and formless beyond my immediate sphere. He only came into focus when I spoke to him, and faded away when he left. I never noticed before." He frowned. "You saw it, didn't you?"

Linnea nodded a confirmation. "I was on the street waiting for you to pass, and everything looked like gray fog. It only lightened and got detailed when you came near me." She shivered. "Kinda creepy, actually."

"I suppose it is," he agreed thoughtfully, "when one is not used to it." He smiled suddenly. "Better stay near me, then—just to be safe."

She laughed, giddy. "An excellent plan. For many reasons."

Supper was bland, served by servants who winked in and out of existence without warning and all looked surprisingly alike. Even Ben seemed disconcerted.

Linnea tried to ignore it—easier to do when the dishes were served and the servants made themselves scarce. Linnea heard the clock striking three as they finished.

"Geez, it's late," she commented.

"Lord, love, I am sorry," Ben returned, getting up with alacrity. "Come—you're exhausted. Let me show you to…" He broke off, chewing on his lip. "Assuming you *have* chambers. I only recall my own."

She chuckled. "Don't worry—it was the middle of the day when I left the real world. I'm going to have fictional jet lag!" she laughed. "And as for the other question… Strathmore?" she said.

The nondescript, stereotypical butler materialized at her elbow. "Yes, Madam?" he intoned.

"Where is my room?"

"Beside Mr. Fortune's. Shall I have the housekeeper show you the way?"

"No, thank you," Linnea answered sunnily, taking Ben's arm. "We'll manage."

"Very good, Madam. When should we expect your luggage and dresser?"

"Uh…" Linnea thought fast. "I do not know *when* my luggage will arrive, and I shall soon be looking to hire a new dresser."

"Very good, Madam. The housekeeper has procured two day dresses for you, and more clothing can be obtained shortly." Linnea noticed that Strathmore hadn't used the housekeeper's name. Maybe, like Strathmore himself, she didn't *have* one until Ben assigned her one? But she would surely be just like Strathmore: the quintessential housekeeper, there to frame Ben Fortune as a man of wealth and status. The clothing would fit perfectly, no doubt, and be appropriate to all possible circumstances: that was how props worked in fiction, unless they were plot points. And these couldn't be, since Linnea wasn't part of the original plot.

"Thank you, Strathmore. Good night."

Ben offered her his arm. "Mrs. Fortune?" He twinkled down at her.

She beamed back. "Lead on, Mr. Fortune."

The stairs seemed to appear as they climbed them, just steps ahead of Ben. At the top was a hallway that stretched in both directions, fading into a sort of gray fuzz at either end. "I am here," Ben told her throwing open the door immediately before them to reveal a large bedroom with a crackling fire and a glimpse of a dressing room beyond. "As my wife, you should be..." A door made itself known nearby. "Here," he said, and in they went.

It was a pretty, feminine room, very ruffled, with a smaller bed, a large wardrobe, a chest, and another fire dancing in the grate. Ben seemed relieved, and somewhat gratified.

A nightrail and dressing gown were laid over the end of the bed, and there was hot water in the ewer. Linnea went over to the wardrobe to see the two day dresses: a pale pink sprigged muslin—far thinner and more delicate than her own, modern muslin—and a pale yellow cotton gown. Both of them would look fantastic with her coloring, thank God.

She turning a smiling face toward Ben. "It's perfect."

He cupped her cheek. "*You're* perfect."

She reached up to kiss him, her heart pounding. "Mm. Do go on."

"I should like to," he began, tucking her close. "God knows I would. But—we are not actually wed, and I would not treat you with so little respect as to assume—"

"Assume what?" she asked breathlessly.

He pressed his lips to her forehead. "That you would welcome my advances."

In response she wrapped her arms around him and lifted her face to be kissed again.

A sound that was somewhere between surrender and possession rumbled low in his chest as he obliged, his mouth hot against hers.

She was lost in his kisses, drugged by the feel of him, the taste. Her body was on fire, her heart yearning.

He groaned again. "Linnea—I don't—I can't—"

Linnea drew back regretfully and tried to smile. "I don't want to press you to do anything you're uncomfortable with."

"It's not—" Ben went unaccountably red. "I should go." He lifted her hand and pressed his lips to her fingers, then turned it over and kissed her palm. "Goodnight, my loveliest, dearest Linnea. I pray you will sleep well." He went slowly to the door and closed it behind him, gazing at her through the gap until the last moment.

The instant the door was shut, it was as if someone had turned out the colors. The room grew gray, amorphous, undetailed. There was a generally fire-like blob in the fireplace-like blob, a foggy ewer on a foggy table, and something that might have passed for a bed to someone who was colorblind and excessively nearsighted.

Linnea shivered. The "fire" was giving little heat or light, and she almost didn't want to touch the bed, for fear her hand would pass right through it. But she straightened her shoulders and went over to the ewer, sticking her hand into it to test the temperature of the water.

It was lukewarm, and when she drew her hand back again, the water clung to her skin and then oozed down her fingers, for all the world as if she were in a cartoon.

That was it. Linnea wrenched the door open and practically fled down the gray hallway to Ben's door.

He turned in surprise as she came barreling in, having just removed his shirt, his breeches half undone, though his boots were still on. He dropped his shirt and caught her instead. "What—what is it?"

"Oh, thank God." This room was detailed and colorful. Of course it was. "As soon as you left the room it went—gray." She shivered again. "I can't sleep in there."

He pulled her into his arms, and she couldn't help remembering that he was half-undressed for bed. Her shiver this time wasn't from fear. "Then you shall not. There is a settee in here—I can take that, and you the bed. Where is your pretty nightrail?"

"It's—in the other room. Will you come with me to get it?"

"Of course." They retrieved the nightrail without incident, Ben also blowing out the candles in Linnea's room, and she was able to change behind a screen in Ben's room while he went into his dressing room to put on his nightshirt, careful not to close the door.

Ben ran the warming pan around under the blankets for her and then took a pillow and blanket to the settee. "Are you sure you can sleep on that?" she said worriedly. It was short, with arms that would require him to sleep in a very cramped position.

He perched himself upon it, head jammed into one arm, bare feet dangling over the other. "Perfectly comfortable," he told her cheerily, waving a hand, and promptly fell off.

Linnea suppressed a chuckle. "Are you all right?"

Ben struggled to his feet. "Fine, thank you. Er—perhaps I shall just make a bed on the floor."

"No, you won't," she said firmly. "This is a big bed. We can share it."

Ben hesitated, fingers clenching reflexively. "Linnea, I—" He cleared his throat. "I love you, you see," as if that explained it all.

Linnea raised her eyebrows and waited.

He took a deep breath. "And—I want you. Which is why—"

"You don't want to be tempted." She took a deep breath. "You know, things are different in my time." He didn't answer, and she tried to lighten the atmosphere. "But if it bothers you, we could find a bundling board," she teased. He merely watched her, as a man upon a precipice, breath coming quickly, eyes dark as night; still he didn't come any closer. Linnea studied him for a moment. "There's something else, isn't there? It's not really about whether we're married, is it?" He hesitated and then shook his head briefly. "What is it, Ben?"

His voice was low. "I—I want to—but… I don't—" He cleared his throat, a flush creeping up his neck. "I know the basic mechanics, but as far as finesse… I have all the practical knowledge of the Regency spinster who invented me. I *ought* to know what to do, how to make desperate, passionate love to you—God knows I feel desperate and passionate enough, but—" He licked his lips. "Will you… teach me?"

The flame inside her roared to a bonfire. She smiled tenderly and reached out her arms to him.

The dark hours before dawn found Ben wide awake, a sleeping Linnea lying loose-limbed in his arms. What was he now? he wondered, a soft smile breaking through his reverie. Fundamentally changed, yes. He could feel it. So very different from the Ben Fortune of Belinda Burnworth's original as to be nearly unrecognizable; different even than he had been yesterday. What had changed?

He kissed the sleeping woman's dark and wavy hair, stifling a chuckle so as not to wake her. Yes, this was rather a startling change, and well beyond anything Miss Burnworth could have imagined, but he rather thought the changes wrought within him were due to his feelings as an independent being, and not just the physical pleasures he and Linnea had shared. Surely the spinster who had invented him—his real mother, so to speak—had never conceived of anything so astonishing as what was between Ben and his lady-love. He had not known such delight was to be had, which meant Miss Burnworth had not, either. But he knew now, which meant he had grown beyond the confines of her imagination. And the love he had for Linnea was not pure esteem, or honor, or any such idealized but remote feeling which his old self might have described. No, indeed. It was deep and strong, filled with faith and forgiveness and joy, tempered with desire and laughter and a sense of... completion.

Linnea shifted in his embrace, murmuring; Ben stroked her hair, caressed her back, until she settled again. This woman… he huffed out a soft sigh. She'd pulled him from his half-life, given him light and color, and risked everything to save him. He could never love her enough, but if she would let him, he'd spend the rest of his life trying.

Dawn was breaking outside his window, and Ben saw, for the first time, that it was like every other dawn he'd experienced here. Not like Linnea's world of infinite variety. No: here the burgeoning sun would streak the sky with pink, shifting to orange toward the north—yes, just like that—before bursting over the horizon, if he were at his estate, or over the London skyline, as now. And just like that it was full morning, with no real passage of time.

Light streamed across his counterpane, caressing Linnea's amber skin, gilding the curve of her throat, her cheek, her dusky lashes and the warm brown cascade of her hair. Ben kissed her forehead. "Good morning, wife," he whispered, his lips against her skin. She mumbled something and shifted, hugging him close. "Linnea, love," he tried again. "It's morning. We should get out of bed," he murmured, though he himself was loath to leave this place of perfect comfort. "The sooner we retrieve Sophia, the sooner we can go home. All of us."

"Mm." She opened her eyes at last and looked up at him. "Home," she repeated, smiling sleepily.

He kissed her mouth, unable to stop himself. "Home," he agreed. Wherever she was, that was his home now.

He escorted her back to her bedroom at last. The phantom housekeeper had sent a housemaid to be her dresser until a proper one could be hired, but Linnea said she didn't want Ben to leave her: she couldn't bear being in the gray space of the narrative again. Far too "creepy." Instead, he helped her with the buttons on her dress. She struggled with putting up her hair, but managed it at last, though the style was very plain.

Ben pressed his lips lightly to the nape of her neck and contemplated her smilingly in the cheval mirror. "You are beautiful, Linnea."

She smiled back at his reflection. "I would have to use curling tongs to get those sausage curls around my face. Oh, well. I don't have to be fashionable." She turned around to kiss him properly. "I just have to not get arrested."

"You need not worry about that," he hastened to assure her. "I believe all is smooth sailing from here. The only difficulty I foresee is explaining the situation to my sister. But she will learn to adjust, as I did. Continue to do," Ben added conscientiously. He gave her another kiss on the temple, and a third on the cheek, the better to get his baser urges under control before heading out to the street: for him, to see Linnea was to want to kiss her. "Are you ready?"

"Ready as I'm going to get!" she answered cheerfully.

Ben had the nebulous Strathmore order the carriage; it pulled up in front of the town house a few moments later, driven by a man whose face was in perpetual three-quarter perspective no matter how Ben tried to view his physiognomy. Shaking his head and trying not to think about it, Ben hoisted a heavy traveling case into the carriage after Linnea. He was briefly stymied by the lack of an actual address for his uncle's house; but "To my uncle's house, and quickly!" seemed to serve well enough, as the carriage set off with a lurch.

Sure enough, they drew up almost immediately at a familiar-looking residence. "Wait here," Ben instructed the faceless coachman, and handed Linnea down from the carriage before bounding up the steps to his uncle's home and pounding on the door.

Strathmore's double answered his knock. "I beg your pardon, sir, but Mr. Moribund Fortune is from home."

"What do you mean, from home?" Ben scowled. "My sister is due to arrive today—he told me so! Surely he is waiting for her."

The butler unbent far enough to allow a miniscule shake of his head. "He departed last evening, after your visit. I believe, sir, he intended to meet her on the post road at Wellmire, to take her on to Rosemont Park, his estate in Herefordshire." Having supplied this much exposition, he closed the door inexorably in Ben's face.

Ben jammed his fingers into his hair, looking at Linnea's lovely countenance in the hopes it would calm him. "*His* estate—he means *my* estate," Ben growled, and then he shook his head. "Are you game for the post road?" he asked her worriedly. "There is no guarantee we will catch them. Time is so strange here. But—I must try."

"Of course," Linnea answered immediately. "But why would he take Sophia to your estate?"

"I don't know. Perhaps he wishes to be out of Town when the news of my untimely demise is reported. Or perhaps he wishes to keep any news of my return from Sophia," Ben ventured, helping her back into the carriage. "Whatever his purpose, I do not trust it. We must make haste to Rosemont Park immediately!" In answer to his words, the coachman's whip cracked, and the carriage set off with the inevitable lurch.

Linnea held onto Ben as the coach swayed quickly around corners. She had the general impression of urban hubbub and traffic outside the vehicle, but she couldn't make out anything specific. At last she could tell that the ground beneath the carriage wheels had shifted from cobblestones to dirt. "Is there any way to look outside?" she ventured.

He nodded, looping up the short shade that covered the window. "There will be dust," he warned, and then frowned slightly. "Probably."

Linnea couldn't see very well through the glass, and realized it could be let down. She did so, and stuck her head out the window.

Things outside the carriage were pretty gray and nebulous. If Linnea leaned out far enough to look ahead, she could see that the landscape lightened, became more colorful, as they approached it, and then faded back into obscurity as they passed it by. Their journey through London had taken less than five minutes, and now they were in the countryside, with dimly-seen hedges and stiles, thatched cottages, and yellow flowers passing in a repetitive parade.

Linnea shivered involuntarily, and put her head back inside the carriage.

Ben put the window back up. "All right, my love?"

Linnea put her hand in his and cuddled up to his side. "Now I am," she smiled up at him. "We'll get out of this okay," she added, as much to herself as to him.

Time skipped, as though within a narrative determined to get to the next event, and without warning the coachman pulled up, horses snorting. Linnea glanced out the window to see that the monotonous scenery had given way to a village setting right out of a Jane Austen film. "Rosebury-on-Wye," Ben confirmed as a perfectly average young man in breeches and a brown coat opened the coach door. "Hello, Stubbins," he greeted the youth, whose visage shifted into individuality as he gave Ben a grin and tugged his forelock.

"Sir," he replied, and helped Linnea down as Ben squinted at the sky. They stood in front of a country inn, and the sun hung directly overhead.

Ben quizzed Stubbins closely about his sister; on receiving confirmation that she had indeed been seen but was hours gone, he turned to Linnea, mouth drawn tight.

"Umm..." Linnea was staring at the coachman and the horses that had drawn them to Rosebury-on-Wye. "Weren't those horses chestnut?" They were now handsome bays.

Ben was looking at her muslin. "They were, and your dress was jonquil when we left." Now it was striped in pink and white. "My clothes have changed as well. The journey from London to Rosemont Park takes more than a day, so I suppose time has... telescoped again, to fit the narrative." He shook himself—or maybe it was a shiver. "All these things I never saw before, and now I find this existence to be unspeakably... what was it? 'Creepy.'"

Linnea nodded fervently. "Let's get something to eat and get moving as soon as we can."

"I must also send some messages," Ben said, his handsome face grim as he lifted his traveling case out of the carriage, apparently averse to leaving it out of his sight in this slightly eldritch conveyance.

"Messages? To whom?"

"The local magistrate. And the militia. I do not know what my uncle has planned, and I have no mind to meet him without defense."

232

The innkeeper, a stereotypically apple-cheeked and jolly personage in a white apron, served them a cold luncheon of meat and bread in a private dining room. Ben jotted out a couple of notes and handed them to the landlord to be delivered immediately, and they were on their way once more.

"To my estate," Ben told the coachman, whose dark queue of hair had been replaced by close-cropped gray curls. Once in the privacy of the carriage, Ben gathered Linnea close, pressing his lips to her brow. "This will be over soon. It must."

Linnea nodded silently.

Sure enough, within minutes they were pulling into a long gravel drive with trees on either side. It was Rosemont Park, just as Burnworth had described it, and with much broader, well-lit vistas than their journey through less specific countryside had offered. Soon they could see the gardens and the imposing neoclassical facade approaching.

Ben was watching out the window, his frown deepening. "But—where are my tenants?" he muttered, under his breath. "I—somehow I *still* thought—" He fell silent, a muscle clenching in his jaw.

Linnea pressed his hand. "Look at it this way," she murmured as the carriage pulled up in front of the broad front steps. "You don't have to worry about what happens to them when we leave again."

He stole a kiss, a warm press of mouth to mouth. "I love you, Linnea. Thank you for pulling me out of this terrible place, for teaching me how to be… real."

She cast him a smile but hadn't time to respond, as a grandly liveried footman opened the door of the carriage.

The beautiful, clean lines of Rosemont Park were before her, and all Linnea could think of was how excited she might have been to see it for herself under other circumstances. There were the rose trellises and the gray stone terrace; the topiary, trimmed into fantastical shapes—all precisely as described by Burnworth.

The butler who opened the front door to them was the triplet to the first two Strathmores. He evinced surprise at their arrival by allowing his brows to move fractionally upward. "Mr. Fortune, sir—I was given to understand—" He paused and pursed his lips. "Mr. Moribund Fortune is in the drawing room, sir. I shall announce you at once."

Ben took Linnea's hand and strode past him. "No need, Stra—" He checked himself, thought about it, then shrugged. "Strathmore. I'll announce myself. Be so good as to prepare chambers for myself and my wife—and see that that case is put in my room," he called over his shoulder.

They passed quickly through the hall, giving Linnea only a moment to note expensive vases, hand-painted wallpaper—and Ben flung open the drawing room door.

The middle-aged man sitting in a chair by the fireplace, in appearance strikingly like his nephew, dropped his brandy snifter in surprise. He blanched visibly, his face taking on a greenish cast. "You!"

The crystal shattered unnoticed upon the hearth as Ben took three long strides across the room and jerked Moribund Fortune from his seat by the lapels. "Where is my sister?" he snarled, right in his uncle's face. "If you have made any unholy plan, if she is harmed in any way—if so much as a single hair on her sweet head is disturbed—"

Moribund's face went from white to red as his shock turned to fury. "How are you here?" he bellowed, shoving Ben away. "I thought I took care of you!"

"Your hired men failed," Ben shouted back, his hands fisting. "*You* have failed in your fell plan, and I intend you shall do so again. Where is Sophia, damn you?"

"How many times do I have to kill you?" Moribund growled, his voice low, and reached for the poker. Linnea swore loudly and dove forward. She hadn't come into fictional Regency England only to see him be attacked by his homicidal uncle! She should have brought her bat.

Moribund caught hold of the poker, and Linnea reached it a split-second after, grappling breathlessly with him for control of the instrument. Ben grabbed at his uncle's throat and drew back his fist.

The sound of a commotion from outside the room froze everyone in place.

"That's quite all right, Strathmore," a female voice—it could hardly be called "feminine" at that low register—boomed down the hall. "We know the way."

"But Madam—!" Strathmore expostulated. "Mr. Fortune is not at home—"

"Nonsense," she thundered again, and the door flung open. Ben sprang back from Moribund, who wrenched the poker from Linnea's grasp and began to poke vigorously at the unlit logs in the hearth.

"Miss Cavanaugh and Miss—uh—Cavanaugh," Strathmore announced meekly, following Araminta and Aunt Virulea into the drawing room.

The scene snapped into full color, full detail. Birds were singing outside the windows in a sunny garden still wet from an overnight rain. Aunt Virulea was huge and magnificent in black bombazine and jet beads, her bulldog-like head held high and her nose broad and thick. Her jowly face was bright red and she was puffing like the Little Engine That Dropped Dead from an Aneurysm.

Beside her, and Linnea had to admit to a certain frisson of perverse excitement about it, was Araminta Cavanaugh, in the flesh. Linnea looked her over, Ben's description in her mind. Her teeth were indeed prominent, but not so bad as Ben had made them sound. Her face was perhaps just a trifle long, and her hair... well, it did have a bit of an ashy tint to it. Her dress was a particularly eye-abrading shade of pink, which might have been the height of fashion but wasn't particularly complimentary to her complexion, and borne on the air

236

that wafted in with them, a faint odor of herbs and gravy. She, too, seemed slightly harried.

Breathless, worried, Linnea glanced over at the others. Ben's shirtpoints had wilted in the humidity, and his face was red with anger, fists still doubled. Moribund had poked the unlit fire as long as he could before the sheer idiocy of the act forced him to turn back to the room and face his guests.

Araminta, Linnea realized, was staring at *her,* eyes narrowed.

"Miss Cavanaugh," Ben said in a voice of strangled surprise, cutting a glance at his uncle, who was doing much the same at him.

Araminta turned toward Ben. "Oh—Mr. Fortune! You have returned! I thought—" She dropped her lashes to signify embarrassment at her unladylike emotional outburst. However, Linea had the distinct impression she wasn't at all surprised to see him here.

"Indeed, the prodigal returns," Moribund replied with some malice. "And with such a lovely, unchaperoned companion, too." The way he looked at Linnea made her skin crawl.

Ben gritted his teeth as he moved to loom next to Linnea. "It is unusual, I believe, for a married couple to require a chaperone. Uncle, Miss Cavanaugh, Miss Araminta: may I present my *wife*, Linnea Fortune." The two men stared each other down.

Araminta was staring at Linnea again, and this time in undisguised horror. "*Wife?*" she repeated.

Aunt Virulea looked even more severe. "Nonsense!" she brayed with all the subtlety and finesse of a canned airhorn blast to the face. "What can you possibly mean by it?"

"I mean," Ben said loudly in return, "to spend the rest of my life with her. That's what's usually meant by the term, I believe."

Virulea gaped, codlike. "But—you—well, I never!" Which was likely the problem, Linnea reflected sourly. The old woman plumped herself down on the settee, bombazine poofing out around her in a black and menacing cloud, redolent of mutton.

Araminta was still gaping like a fish, staring back and forth between Ben and Linnea, Finally she shut her mouth, though she turned as pink as her gown, which was probably as uncomfortable a process as it looked. "Oh, I do congratulate you," she enthused suddenly, coming forward to shake Linnea's hand briefly. Linnea raised a brow. So that was how she was going to play it. "But how very secretive of you, Mr. Fortune!" Araminta fawned. "So that is where you have been these weeks!"

"It is." He took Linnea's hand and led her to the settee facing Virulea, kissing her fingers reverently as she took a seat. "I have been discovering and securing my greatest happiness, and have come home only for the blessings of friends and family before my *wife* and I," he seemed to say that word with great relish, "and my sister Sophia, return to the Americas."

Moribund's scowl at this proclamation was prodigious.

Araminta fluffed down next to her aunt and tittered unbecomingly. "America! Is that where you hail from, Miss—*Mrs.* Fortune?"

The excuse seemed as good as any. "Yes, as a matter of fact," Linnea answered.

Virulea flapped open a great black fan and began to raise a small tornado with it. "La, sir," she said, all of a sudden terrifyingly playful, "to leave us all in such suspense! What can you have been thinking? No," she reached across the tea table and rapped his knuckles as though with a blackjack. Ben winced. "It is too monstrous cruel of you. But we must forgive you, I suppose. Of course you will have a ball for them?" She turned on Moribund, who flinched visibly, while Ben surreptitiously rubbed the back of his hand. Virulea's gaze darted back to Linnea. "I suppose they *do* such things in America? It's not all wild natives and scalpings every moment?"

"Not at all," Linnea answered, sitting up as tall as she could and giving Aunt Virulea a proud stare.

Apparently pleased to have got a barb home, Virulea went on. "Of course, my Araminta would perish in such a place, I am sure, so fragile and pale a blossom as she is. You must be made of much... *sterner* stuff, Mrs. Fortune. Ancestors among the hidalgos, I imagine? Or perhaps you yourself have native blood, to flourish in such an uncivilized clime?"

Moribund snickered; Ben got up suddenly and trod on his foot, hard enough to make the older man yelp. "Oh, that *was* clumsy of me. Do forgive me, Uncle. My *wife*," Ben replied with unholy glee as the old lady made a moue of displeasure, "has a most unique and beautiful heritage indeed. Spanish, as you presume, by way of Puerto Rico. American, by birth. And now English, by consent, bless her. In her you see the Western world in most perfect harmony," he added, gazing at her lovingly.

"Well, if that's how you choose to look at it," Virulea sniffed disdainfully. Linnea and Ben ignored her.

Instead, Ben pinned his uncle with a darkling look. "And my sister, sir? Though it is always a delight to renew old acquaintance," he gave the Cavanaughs a nod, "Sophia is the reason my wife and I have traveled so far. I should like Linnea to know her new sister as soon as possible. Where is she?"

Moribund shifted uncomfortably. "In her room, I make no doubt. She was not well when last I saw her."

Ben's frown was mighty indeed, his eyes narrowing. "I'm sure she will be all the better for seeing her family. Strathmore!"

The butler hove into sight. "Sir?"

"Kindly ask my sister to join us, will you?"

"Sir." He faded from view again.

An awkward silence descended. "Beautiful country," Linnea suggested.

240

Araminta began to agree, but Virulea cut her off. "Rustication and ruin," she proclaimed, rolling her R's. "We would have done better to stay in Town."

"Oh, but country air is so beneficial," Linnea answered in her best Regency manner.

Virulea dug around in her reticule, coming up with a lorgnette, with which she viewed Linnea before hmphing a comprehensive hmph. "The pleasures of Town life far outweigh the dubious attractions of the country, and so I was just telling my darling Araminta." Her niece looked bewildered, but nodded loyally. "Indeed, we shall return to London this very week, since our holiday has proved so unfruitful."

Linnea bit her lips to keep from grinning. Translation: Now that Fortune's taken.

A flurry in the hallway, and then a slight girl tumbled into the room, her wide eyes as blue as the dress she wore, her hair black as a raven's wing. "Ben? Oh—oh, *Ben!*" Sophia threw herself into her brother's strong arms.

This time Linnea's smile was full-hearted. The two embraced movingly, and when they drew back to regard one another, Linnea thought she detected tears in both their eyes. Ben cupped his sister's face, pressing his lips to her forehead. "I know, I know, I'm sorry," he murmured in answer to her urgent whispers. She curled her fingers around his lapels, leaning her face against his waistcoat with a shuddering sigh. "But I shall not leave without you again, Sophy, I promise. Now, let me introduce you to Linnea."

Sophia, after an uncertain look at Ben's face, presented herself to her new "sister-in-law" with a curtsey.

Linnea gave her a broad smile and came forward with her hands out. "Sophia. I've heard so much about you."

The girl blushed, though she took Linnea's hands readily. "My brother does me too much credit, I feel sure. Welcome to Rosemont Park... sister." Sophia smiled suddenly, looking very much like her brother. "I have always longed for a sister," she finished shyly.

"So have I," Linnea assured her. Sophia blushed again and retired to stand behind Ben, though her eyes were as bright as her cheeks. After a moment she reached for his hand, and the two siblings drew a little away from the group, their voices very low as they spoke. At one point Ben looked up at Linnea with such emotion in his gaze it stole her breath; at nearly the same moment she felt the oddest prickling on the back of her neck, and turned back to the Misses Cavanaugh, the elder of whom currently had her lorgnette homed in on Linnea's bare left hand.

After digging her elbow into her wincing niece's side as though excavating for gold, Virulea cleared her throat ('CHUG-A-RUM', as Grandfather Toad used to say in the books Linnea had read as a child), and blared, "Mr. Fortune!"

Both Ben and Moribund swiveled their heads to look at her, the first with an air of faint exasperation, the latter with a flavor of terrified disgust. Virulea smiled,

242

which did nothing to ameliorate her aura of menace. "We," she announced triumphantly, "shall stay to dinner."

This was a bridge too far, even for poor Araminta, who went absolutely cerise. "Aunt—" she protested, but was stared down. The girl fidgeted, but subsided, though her eyes as she sought Linnea's gaze held what looked like apology.

Moribund's mouth worked for nearly a full five seconds before he could bring himself to speak. "Of course," he managed finally, his voice thin and raspy. "Wouldn't dream of anything else. Would we, nephew?"

Why was the older man going with this? He seemed intimidated by Virulea, and wouldn't it be easier to attack Ben again if she weren't there, watching his every move? But they all knew now that Ben *hadn't* simply died conveniently in the anonymous streets of fictional London, Linnea realized, so Moribund's opportunity was already gone. Virulea and Araminta could inform against him if Ben disappeared now from his own home—not to mention the public scandal.

That was it. Moribund Fortune didn't have any prospect of obtaining the family money anymore. He probably lived entirely off of reputation and credit, and couldn't afford to alienate even such a gorgon as Virulea Cavanaugh if he wanted that credit to continue.

Meanwhile, Virulea had apparently smelled a rat, and was determined to get to the bottom of it.

Ben's lips had thinned, but he seemed unwilling to make a scene, too. With a start Linnea recalled something which he had clearly never quite forgotten: in Araminta's presence, they had an audience—not just Virulea Cavanaugh, but however many millions of avid readers were watching the book anxiously back in the real world, waiting to see what would happen next.

Kurt made as if to throw the book across the room in frustration, but Susan caught his arm. "Will you *quit* that? If you're going to throw a tantrum every time Virulea says something, give the book to me and let me do the reading."

He gave her the book, scowling. Rose broke in. "It's not Virulea," she pointed out to her girlfriend, who was rummaging for the page. "It's that Ben and Linnea are stuck, as long as Araminta's there. They can't leave in front of her."

"Yeah," Susan agreed on an exhale of breath. "I know."

Nadine patted Kurt's broad shoulder, then leaned over Susan's. "The change in Araminta is interesting, though." The other three looked at her with varying expressions of 'What are you on about?', and she shrugged, going a little pink. "Well—she's clearly embarrassed by Virulea's antics. Shows a bit of self-awareness, don't you think?" A long silence ensued, during which Kurt's brow rose slowly. "I'm just saying," Nadine replied defensively, "that the tone of the book has changed. Araminta's not so bad after all."

Susan summed up the group's feelings succinctly. "Who *cares?* She needs to get the hell out of there so Ben and Linnea can come back!"

The air between them all was constrained as they sat down to dinner. Araminta could not help but notice the glares of hatred Mr. Moribund Fortune kept directing toward his nephew, nor the way Miss Fortune's eyes kept straying from her brother's face to that of her new sister-in-law with something akin to wonder. Was Sophia as surprised at this sudden romance as Araminta herself? Or was there some other cause?

Aunt Virulea was continuing in a strain Araminta found most painful. She was hurt to find that Ben had preferred another woman to herself, and would have been glad to return to her aunt's house to have some time to herself. But Aunt Virulea was still plotting, and now she was clearly attempting to embarrass this strange, rather swarthy young woman who had interrupted her schemes.

"My dear Mrs. Fortune." Aunt Virulea had a way of pronouncing certain words to give them the precisely opposite meaning, and she employed it now. Araminta tried not to draw her aunt's ire by visibly wincing. "In what parish were you wed? What day? What church? What clergyman?" The elder Miss

245

Cavanaugh fired off her questions like an infantryman who needed no time to reload. "I see you have forgot your ring," she added with something like smugness, though surely Aunt would never stoop so low in feeling.

"Son of a—" Kurt exploded and began rolling up his sleeves.

"What do you think you're doing?" Susan asked him, marking the place in the novel as she paused.

"Okay, first of all," he held up a finger, "*swarthy?* Really? We're going there?"

"It's the setting," Nadine protested. "You can't blame Araminta for the prejudices of an entire era."

"The hell I can't. And secondly: Auntie Influenza is onto them. Somebody needs to warn them, and maybe take out that crappy Uncle Mortimer as well." Kurt was pacing the room.

"Moribund," Rose corrected him.

He shot her a look. "Whatever. I'll go in, pop him one, shove the witch out the window, and bring Ben and Linnea home. And his sister, too."

Nadine looked shocked. "But—the novel! You can't just destroy it! What about Araminta?"

Kurt rounded on her. "Araminta and the novel can go—" here he described something that would end in some very uncomfortable paper cuts. "She's *fictional*, Professor. Ben and Linnea aren't."

The professor leveled him a look. "Are you so sure about that? Araminta comes from the same place as

246

Ben does, and as you say, he's real enough—and he wasn't even the main character in the book. Do you really believe you have the right to ruin Araminta's life? Her world?"

"To save my friends?" Kurt folded his arms. "Hell yeah."

"But so far all they're in danger of is a delay," Nadine argued. "The militia is on its way. Let the plot play out. If it goes badly, we'll go in and correct it, whatever it is. But for now, let it play out, please."

After a moment spent gritting his teeth, Kurt agreed with a bad grace, flinging himself back onto the sofa. "Keep reading, then," he told Susan grumpily.

The old lady peppered Linnea with questions calculated to catch her off her guard. Linnea studied Aunt Virulea for a moment: this awful, smelly old woman who thought her less than she was. Linnea stifled a smile. She'd been fielding this kind of prejudice practically from birth. "Oh, we were married by special license," she answered airily. Time to see if she could give Virulea some of her own medicine. She cast Ben an uncharacteristically flirtatious smile, gazing at him through her lashes. He practically inhaled his wine and began coughing, his ears going red. Linnea laughed to herself. "I'm afraid we hadn't time to procure a ring."

Virulea choked on her tea. "No time? What can you mean?" She dabbed at her bombazine-covered prow, raising narrowed eyes to Linnea. "You think to shock me, gel. I warn you, I am not so easily put off."

"Aunt!" Araminta whispered frantically.

Linnea suddenly realized that, according to the etiquette of Regency England, she was the Lady of the House. She put down her napkin and rose. "Shall we retire, ladies?"

The two men rose and bowed as the ladies prepared to leave the room. Virulea harrumphed and got to her feet, which was something like watching the QEII go into drydock. Head up, Linnea led the way, accompanied by gasping trout noises and disgruntled snuffling from the elder Miss Cavanaugh. "I fail to see," Virulea was arguing as she shouldered past the other three ladies, "why we should not have the company of the gentlemen for a quarter-hour in such a small party. Surely, in such congenial company, we need not be so… rigorous." This last word was rolled out with relish, accompanied by the snap of her lorgnette as she sailed triumphantly past Linnea into the drawing room.

A thump from behind them caught Linnea's attention, followed by a masculine grunt. She turned to glimpse Ben dodging his uncle's fist. He grabbed it and twisted the older man's arm, spinning him around to shove him into the wall. Linnea opened her mouth to protest—

"MR. FORTUNE!" Virulea trumpeted like an elephant calling to its mate across a particularly rowdy stretch of the Serengeti.

Ben appeared, breathless, a moment later, his neckcloth completely skewed to the side. "Ma'am?" Moribund loomed behind him, a streak of dust on his face.

The old virago's lips stretched into a grotesquely complacent smile. "Come, you need not dawdle over your port, or whatever it is you men do," she said archly, her lashes fluttering like a coquettish lizard's. "Surely you do not intend to neglect your guests?"

Ben's own well-cut mouth twisted; after a moment he managed, "Of course not, Miss Cavanaugh." Behind him, his uncle's scowl deepened, but the two men followed the ladies into the drawing room.

Linnea took the opportunity to straighten Ben's neckcloth, only partially because of the expression of outrage it provoked on Virulea's jowly, ruddy face. "Are you all right?" Linnea murmured, making rather a business of tidying him up.

His gaze as she looked up into his face was warm indeed. "Fine. I've thirty years and three stone on the man. And the militia should be here soon."

Virulea harrumphed her indignation at having to witness a married couple (so far as she knew) behaving like a married couple. "If you have quite finished valeting your *husband*, madam?"

Araminta winced at this emphasis. "Surely, Aunt," she began. "I do think—"

"Well, you should not, my gel. It is not a skill you possess." Virulea turned her lorgnette on her niece, who got up suddenly and crossed to where Sophia stood by the fireplace.

Strathmore made an unexpected entrance, distracting everyone from the cloud of awkwardness that had settled thickly about them. "Sir—Mr. Fortune?" he began, looking from Ben to Moribund and back.

"Yes?" they answered in unison, each glaring at the other.

"Lord Frumpington has arrived, and brought with him some *persons*," Strathmore said feelingly before melting away.

Ben smirked; Moribund frowned. "Persons?" snapped the latter.

"Militia," Ben clarified gleefully. "You're finished, old man."

Moribund stared at him, eyes first widening and then narrowing, his face darkening into a hatred that made Linnea's hair stand on end. In a moment, Moribund had pulled a pistol from his pocket and grabbed Linnea's wrist. "If you try to take me, she dies!" he snarled.

But Linnea had taken a self-defense course from a Krav Maga instructor. She spread her hand and jerked her arm in a quick circle, breaking his grip.

Moribund swore and lunged at her, throwing his arm around her throat and dragging her backward. Linnea drove her elbow into his solar plexus and her heel into his kneecap. He howled in pain, there was a deafening report, and Sophia screamed. Ben staggered backward with a grunt, and then there was a loud *thump*.

Linnea turned to see Moribund's eyes crossing. His face went slack, and he toppled onto his face to reveal Araminta standing behind him, holding the fireplace poker aloft, an expression of horrified satisfaction on her face.

Susan stared at Kurt. "You did *not* just stop there. Was Ben *shot*?" She launched herself across the sofa, climbing his lanky body for the book. "Give me that!"

"Hey—hey!" Kurt protested, holding *Fortune's Folly* aloft as he slapped her hands away. "I didn't do it on purpose! The rest is still in flux!"

"GIMME!" Susan wrestled for possession of the paperback; they both fell off the sofa in a welter of limbs.

Rose was thumbing through her phone, munching on a cookie. "Tweeter just blew up," she observed. "It's not just us—the situation's not resolved yet."

Nadine reached over to the struggling pair and plucked the book from Kurt's hand, earning a howl of protest from both combatants. She examined the pages. "Still morphing. Be patient," she advised. "If it goes wrong, I'll go in and fix it. I'm the one with the costume," she added, when the other three seemed disposed to argue. "And I've been in there before. Just wait a little longer."

Linnea ran for Ben, calling his name desperately. "Are you okay?" she cried.

He was clutching his arm, crimson seeping through his fingers. "A graze only, I think," he gritted.

Araminta dropped the poker from nerveless fingers as the door burst open and three men rushed in, Strathmore on their heels. Two of the newcomers were in uniform, and these took custody of the dazed and cursing Moribund. The third addressed Ben. "'Pologies for the delay, Mr. Fortune. Would've been here sooner, but m'horse threw a shoe, stupid animal." Lord Frumpington pursed his lips, looking at Ben's wound. "No aim. Good thing."

"Strathmore, some water and bandages?" Linnea said, her voice still high-pitched with fear.

The butler disappeared, hopefully to do her bidding. Across the room, Sophia began to cry; Araminta went to the girl, folding her close. Virulea lay practically prostrate on the sofa, a large, frilly handkerchief covering her ruddy face, her bosom heaving.

The magistrate caught sight of her. "Alright there, Miss C?" he called bracingly.

"I have *never*," managed Aunt Virulea weakly, the hanky flopping wildly with the force of her whisper, "*never*, in my life, been exposed to such ignominy."

Lord Frumpington's lips twitched. "Strathmore," he said blandly as the butler reentered in

252

record time with the bandages, "a drink and some smelling salts for Miss Cavanaugh."

Virulea lifted the corner of her handkerchief. "Brandy," she specified, and let the cloth fall again.

"Don't fuss, love," Ben protested as Linnea began to ease him out of his coat. "I'm fine. See to Sophy, will you?"

After making sure it really was just a graze, Linnea acquiesced. She gave him a pad of bandages to press to the wound, and went to his sister.

Sophia went from Araminta's arms to Linnea's. "Ben—is Ben going to die?" she asked piteously.

"Ben's going to be just fine," Linnea crooned, hugging the girl tightly. "It's just a scratch. Everything's going to be fine."

Sophia shuddered and nodded, hiding her face against Linnea's shoulder. Araminta, after a hesitation, touched Linnea's arm lightly, a tentative smile on her face, and then she turned to her aunt, who was demanding more brandy. "Aunt," Araminta announced in a no-nonsense tone, "we must go."

Virulea paused, a steam-whistle cut off mid-shriek. "I will *not* be spoken to in that tone—"

Araminta, a delicate vision in screaming cerise, strode to the settee and put her aunt in a reasonably efficient armlock, hauling her to her feet. "Now, Aunt. We have overstayed our welcome, I am afraid."

Lord Frumpington eyed the young woman with new appreciation. "I'll need your statement regarding these events, Miss Araminta."

"You may collect it at Cavanaugh Hall at your leisure, sir," she replied with an awkward curtsey. "Just now I am afraid my aunt is overset and requires the comfort of familiar surroundings. Will you excuse us?"

"Araminta," Linnea said as the young woman steered her aunt toward the door.

She looked back, that tentative smile trembling her lips again. "Yes, Mrs. Fortune?"

"Thank you," Linnea replied, smiling back. "For everything."

Araminta's own smile broadened, softening her features into something approaching beauty. "You are most welcome, I am sure. Farewell, Mrs. Fortune, Mr. Fortune, Miss Fortune. Come, Aunt."

They could hear Virulea baying in protest all the way out to the drive.

Chapter Fourteen

Linnea went back to Ben, helping him off with his shirt and bathing and bandaging the graze. "We'll get Kurt to look at it when we get back," she promised.

They went through the formalities of making their statements to Lord Frumpington, Sophia huddled at her brother's side, while the militiamen secured Moribund. He remained stonily silent throughout; at last they took the prisoner away, and Linnea was left alone with the two Fortunes.

"You should probably explain where you've been," Linnea murmured to Ben.

He nodded and gave Sophy a squeeze. "We're going on an adventure, Kitten."

She looked up at him. "To America?"

"Yes—and no," Ben temporized. "America, certainly. But not the one you've heard about. We're going to the *real* America, and it's nothing like anything you ever dreamed of."

Sophy's forehead puckered. "The... *real* America? What can you mean?"

Ben glanced at Linnea and then ran his fingers through his hair, setting his dark curls all askew while he blew out a breath. "This is going to sound mad, Sophia. You'll think I'm fit for nothing more than Bedlam. But—I implore you to trust me." He inhaled deeply. "Have you ever read a book and imagined it to be real?"

She was bewildered by this. "Yes, of course."

He nodded and took the plunge, telling her the whole story. Well—not the *whole* story, Linnea thought with a frisson of pleasure, recalling their private time in London. Some things it was better not to share.

Sophia seemed, by turns, disbelieving, frightened, and somewhat exhilarated. "If you tell me it is so," she said at last, breathlessly, "then—then I must believe you. You would not lie to me so." Still she looked at Linnea, her expression beseeching.

"It's true," she confirmed. "Every word. We're going back to the real world—to twenty-first-century America—and we want you to come with us."

The younger girl's bright eyes were round. "Will we ever come back?"

Ben looked steadily at Linnea, though he spoke to his sister. "No, Kitten. We're going to stay there and be happy, for the rest of our lives."

Linnea smiled back at him. *For the rest of our lives.*

"Happy," Sophia breathed, and laced her fingers through her brother's. "I have not been, without you.

256

Where you go," she said stoutly, "I go too. I am not afraid. Much," she added, biting her lip.

"That's my girl." He stroked the back of his finger down her cheek, and then got to his feet. "We should go, hm? I know you have questions, and I'll answer them all, but—I'd rather not tempt fate. What if Virulea comes back?" Ben chuckled. "I just need to get my valise." He kissed Linnea's forehead. "Wait here."

As he left, the immediate environs greyed out some. Not entirely, as Sophia had been a minor point-of-view character in Burnworth's original notes, Linnea concluded. But enough that it was eerie, nonetheless.

Sophia seemed to notice this effect for the first time, blue eyes wide. "What is happening? The walls... I have never before noticed..."

"Yeah. Creepy, huh?" Linnea took her hand. "But where we're going, that never happens. You'll see."

The young woman nodded absently, watching her surroundings with a kind of terrified fascination. Soon Ben reappeared, the room brightening instantly. He tapped the case. "Ready," he said with a smile. "Is there anything else we must do here?"

"I think we're ready," Linnea answered

He nodded and put an arm about each of them, wincing just a bit. "Not a moment too soon, in my opinion. Say the words, my love."

Linnea recited the return spell.

It was as if the lights had come up. They were flooded with color and detail and sound.

"Hey!" Kurt levered up from the sofa, tossed his paperback into the air, and jogged over to them, throwing his arms around Linnea. "'Bout time!"

Sophia shrank back, squinting, a hand held up as though to ward off all this new input.

Linnea laughed, hugging him back. "Everybody, meet Sophia! ...Let's not overwhelm her, hm?" she added warningly.

The others gathered around, Susan hugging Linnea and Ben effusively. "Your arm!" she exclaimed to Ben. "Kurt, do something!"

"Ease *up*, woman, geez." He shouldered her out of the way while Nadine took charge of Sophia, leading her to the sofa.

Rose slipped an arm around Linnea's waist while the other two fussed over Ben. "Come on, you sit too. You must be wiped," she sympathized. "That was quite a thing to watch—must have been crazy to live it."

"Oh my God, you have no idea. Fiction-land is creepy as hell."

"Yeah?" Rose offered her a cookie. "Do tell."

So Linnea described the watery grayness of the novel whenever a point-of-view character wasn't present, and then told the story of their adventures, most of which weren't visible to the readers, who only got Araminta's side of the story.

Nadine leaned forward, Sophia clutching her hand. "The archives—my archives—changed too," she said with a meaningful nod. "Those letters are gone."

Linnea slumped back, puffing her cheeks out with a sigh of relief. "Thank God. Everything fixed."

Rose slanted a glance at the trio in the kitchenette, where Kurt was debating loudly with Susan over whether Ben's injury would require stitches. "So," the blonde said with a grin. "*Mrs.* Fortune, huh?"

Linnea grinned and felt herself go pink. "We had to say that. Otherwise we couldn't travel together alone."

Sophia was bewildered by this. "You—you are *not* married? But—"

"Not *yet*," contributed Ben from the kitchen, and Kurt and Susan high-fived each other. Linnea laughed and pressed her hands to her burning cheeks.

Sophia gave a small smile.

"Well, I think this calls for celebration!" Rose announced.

The others agreed with alacrity, and Kurt got out wine glasses while Ben excused himself to change out of his Regency clothing. He returned a few minutes later in his favorite Doctor Who t-shirt and the jeans Linnea liked best on him. Sophia stared at her brother, blue eyes wide.

He went to sit beside her, taking her hands in his. "You see, Kitten, everything is different here. You'll learn, just as I did. And we'll help you." Ben looked at each of them in turn. "We all will."

She looked trustingly up at him. "It's very colorful," she offered with a shy smile.

He laughed, slipping an arm around her shoulders. "It is. And loud, and bewildering. And wonderful." Kurt passed around the glasses, and Ben raised his. "To life," he grinned. "And the freedom to live it."

"To life!" they all chorused, and drank.

"So... where's my baseball bat?" Kurt poked Linnea, who laughed. They got very rowdy after that, talking over one another, laughing and joking. Even Sophia got into the spirit, making a few observations on Virulea's behavior. Only Nadine seemed thoughtful.

Linnea nudged Ben, who put down his glass and regarded the older woman. "Is there something amiss, Professor?"

"I was just thinking about Araminta," she said slowly. "It seems to me that she really helped you out there at the end."

"She did, indeed," he agreed. "I would not have thought it in her, but... it's clear I underestimated her. I hope that, however her story ends, it ends well."

"That's just what I was thinking," Nadine answered. "And I'd—like to help her to find that happy ending."

"What do you mean?" Linnea asked.

Nadine straightened her shoulders. "I want to go into the book."

Linnea almost dropped her glass. *"Fortune's Folly?"*

"Fortune's Folly. Yes." Nadine nodded. "You said," she pointed out to Ben, "that Araminta was... very

hard to take—probably a result of how Burnworth originally wrote her. Nonetheless, she seems to have improved. And thousands of *Fortune's Folly* fans have seen in her over the years something better than what Burnworth apparently did. That version of Araminta must be in her somewhere. I want to help her find it."

Kurt objected loudly. "Aw, hell no. I am not going to sit around getting another ulcer while you crazy people go book-hopping. Today was bad enough."

"Hold on, though." This was Rose, thoughtful. "There's no threat—Moribund's done for. As long as you don't mess with the part of the narrative Ben and Linnea just went through... why not?"

"Why not indeed?" Nadine nodded decisively. "I will enter the story immediately after the point of your departure, then."

Ben's winged brows drew together as he considered. "I could write you a power of attorney," he said slowly. "Appoint you trustee over my lands and funds; then you would have the wherewithal to move in the correct circles. But—your life here? Your position at the college—would you endanger that, to aid Araminta?"

Nadine grinned. "How much time did you spend in the book, Linnea?"

"Um... two days? Three?"

"And how much time was that out here?" she asked the rest of the room at large.

"Several hours," Susan answered.

"Well, there's your answer. I'll come back out when I need to, and then I can go right back in where I left off. I would appreciate that power of attorney," she added to Ben. "Thank you."

"Well, I'm glad to know your little vacation won't harm my dissertation writing," Susan grinned.

Nadine laughed. "Never fear, I'll be back and forth. You'll hardly notice I'm gone. Won't even ask you to take over my classes." She grinned impishly at her.

Linnea produced pen and stationery from her desk, and Ben began to write. "What name shall I give you? 'Bialecki' will raise too many eyebrows. Even 'Nadine' is quite unusual for my time."

"Eulalie Crabtree," Nadine chuckled, after a moment's thought.

"Eulalie Crabtree it is!" Ben grinned. Nadine dashed into the bathroom to change back into her Regency costume. Ben had Kurt and Rose witness his letter to his attorney, and also jotted out instructions to Strathmore and servants and a letter of introduction to Araminta.

The professor read this latter missive aloud. "*My dear Miss Cavanaugh,*" she began. "*You have proved so good and steadfast a friend to me and to my family that I take the liberty of introducing to your notice one who will, I feel sure, perform the same offices for you. I send you every wish and hope for your continued health and happiness. Your servant—and friend—Ben Fortune.* Thank you!" Nadine enthused. "This should answer beautifully."

"If it doesn't," Ben cautioned her, "you must return immediately. Take no chances, please."

"I won't," the professor promised. "Oh—here." She handed him her house keys. "You and Sophia can stay at my place—we'll call it exchange housesitting." She began leafing through the end of the book.

"Wait, you're going *now*?" Susan echoed everyone's surprise.

Nadine grinned. "Are you kidding? I can't *wait*! See you at some point!" With that she uttered the spell and disappeared.

Sophia clapped her hands in delight and laughed. "I *like* this world!"

The party went late into the night, punctuated by the occasional announcement of how Tweeter and the media in general were reacting to all the changes to the novel. The fact that Ben Fortune had married, and had married a woman of color, no less, seemed to dumbfound some people and delight others. At about two in the morning, Susan picked up the copy of the novel into which Nadine had so recently disappeared. "Uh—guys?"

Heads swiveled. "What? What is it?" Kurt asked anxiously. "I knew this was going to give me an ulcer. Somebody get me the Pepto. Did Aunt Virulea finally snap? Is the Prof okay?"

"No, it's—um—" She held the book up so that they could see the front cover.

There was a stunned silence. "She changed the *title?*" Rose squeaked.

Sure enough, the novel now proudly proclaimed its new name: *Araminta.*

Ben smiled. "No longer my folly. It's fully her story now. As it ought always to have been."

Susan was flipping through the pages, which seemed to be slowly multiplying under her hands. "Looks like Nadine's doing a great job," she said, then laughed. "She's disarming Virulea on every second word! Go Nadine!"

Linnea laughed and stretched. "I can't wait to read it. Or rather, I can. Until tomorrow afternoon, when I'm actually awake."

"We can drive you guys to Nadine's," Rose offered Ben and Sophia.

Kurt went to get Ben's traveling case. "Oof! What do you have in here—rocks?"

Ben chuckled and hefted it up onto the coffee table. "Of a kind." He popped open the buckles. "I couldn't let you and Linnea keep supporting me, so I took a little visit to the bank, and..." He flipped open the lid of the case. Inside sat dozens of flat boxes, neatly stacked one against the other. "Pick one," he invited Linnea, a broad smile on his handsome face.

Confused, she pointed to one. "Um... that one?"

Ben picked it up and opened it, lifting a dazzling diamond and ruby necklace from its bed of velvet, and held it to Linnea's throat. Sophia clasped her hands. "Great-grandmother's parure!"

Linnea's eyes felt like they were bulging out of her head. "Are they ALL like that?" she squeaked.

He grinned. "Of course."

With a muffled exclamation, Susan reached for a box, then checked herself. "May I?"

"Of course," Ben said again, and stepped back as the women dove in eagerly.

"OH MY GOD," Susan shrieked, pulling out a tiara. "INSTAGRAPH ME, ROSE. INSTAGRAPH ME IMMEDIATELY."

"Instagraph me like one of your French girls!" Rose answered, pulling out a huge sapphire on a silver chain.

"You're going to sell these?" Linnea asked Ben.

"Most of them, yes. Some of the jewels are Sophy's, to do with as she likes," he clarified. "And— somewhere in here—" Ben rummaged around and finally came up with a small box. "This is—" He stopped and slipped the box in his pocket. "For later," he added with a smile.

Rose gave a squeal and clapped her hands over her mouth. Linnea laughed and blushed and kept looking at the jewels. "Oh, and you brought the records of sale with you too—good idea. The provenance will make them more valuable."

Kurt suddenly sat up very straight. "WAIT WAIT WAIT!"

The others all stared at him. "What?"

"Are you saying…" Kurt pinned Ben with a look. "You're telling me that you brought priceless jewels out of a fictional novel—and they're *real?*"

Ben raised his brows. "Sophia and I am, why should they not be? I brought no currency, as that would be meaningless; art, too, since its value lies in the fame of the artist, and my world and yours may not coincide that way. But this seemed a safe bet."

Kurt grabbed his head frantically. "But—you guys—" Suddenly he jumped up, vaulted over the back of the sofa, and ran to his room, where they could hear him crashing about and cursing. Susan raised her brows at Linnea, who shrugged.

He returned moments later, panting, a book in his hands. "Don't you get it?" He held up the book, tapping the cover, depicting a pirate burying a chest, overflowing with gold and jewels: Robert Louis Stevenson's *Treasure Island*. "Guys," he said, excitement thrumming through his voice: "*I can pay off my student loans!*"

Fin

www.ingramcontent.com/pod-product-compliance
Lightning Source LLC
Chambersburg PA
CBHW031304170626
46807CB00001B/311